MARIE MERRITT—her broken heart drives her into the arms of a man she discovers she can never love—for a totally devastating reason.

MARK BROOKS—a young doctor with a shattered past, he reaches out to Marie and is caught up in one of fate's cruelest tricks.

BILL HORTON—haunted by seeing the woman he loves married to his brother, his ceaseless torment becomes violent revenge.

KITTY HORTON—her return to Salem means trouble for everyone—but the price *she* will pay will be the highest.

P9-CAN-407

Series Story Editor **Mary Ann Cooper** is America's foremost soap opera expert. She writes the nationally syndicated column *Speaking of Soaps,* is a major contributor to leading soap opera magazines, and is a radio and television personality.

Besides being a novelist, writer **Gilian Gorham** is a widely published poet. She divides her time between her Manhattan penthouse and her cottage in Beverly Hills.

Dear Friend,

We all know two friends like Julie Olson and Susan Hunter. They pledge undying friendship until a man comes along to drive them apart, making them bitter enemies for life.

But Julie and Susan escalate their hatred for one another beyond the bedroom and into courtrooms and jail cells. As a result, Susan becomes strangely demented by her jealousy of Julie. And Julie sadly loses sight of everything she once held dear to her as the result of Susan's vindictive actions. As in most cases, innocent people suffer as a result.

Here in Book 3, *Search for Love*, we learn the reason why revenge is never really sweet. Book 4, *Sentimental Longings*, tells us that this is really just the beginning of the bitterness between Susan and Julie. The question is—where will it all end?

For Soaps & Serials Books,

Mary Ann Cooper

Mary Ann Cooper

P.S. If you missed Books 1 and 2 of this series, see the order form on page 192 which also tells you how to order books in our other Soaps & Serials™ paperback series.

DAYS OF OUR LIVES

SEARCH FOR LOVE

PIONEER COMMUNICATIONS NETWORK, INC.

Search For Love

DAYS OF OUR LIVES paperback novels are published and distributed by Pioneer Communications Network, Inc.

SOAPS & SERIALS™ is a trademark of Pioneer Communications Network, Inc.

ISBN: 0-916217-53-1

Printed in the United States of America

10 9 8 7 6 5 4 3 2 1

SEARCH FOR LOVE

Chapter One
Rock-a-bye Baby

Dr. Laura Spencer sat at her desk poring over a series of glossy eight-by-ten photographs that could have come out of a lurid crime magazine. One showed the corpse of a young man lying in a thick pool of blood, his face partially disfigured by shotgun blasts. Others showed the body from various angles. Close-ups even picked out the pattern of an expensive Oriental rug beneath the body. Indeed, the elegant decor suggested both money and taste. But the young man who had been blown away by a shotgun looked as if he had been the victim of murder committed by thugs in the back alley of a sordid slum.

And a shotgun was the weapon—there was no doubt about that. There were more pictures showing the formidable double-gauged instrument of death, which looked powerful enough to hold off an army of grizzly bears.

Finally Laura flipped through the photographs of the "alleged perpetrator"—to use the police parlance—being led off to jail. She was a young woman, tall and big-boned, with wild, wiry blond hair, uncombed and sticking out in all directions. She was dressed in the cut-off jeans and sandals. The young woman was Susan Martin, and although Laura Spencer did not know her as well as she would have liked to, she knew her a great deal better than either the police or the district attorney did.

The urgent question confronting Laura now was, could her knowledge about the defendant help Susan Martin escape a verdict of murder in the second degree? Susan's attorney, Mickey Horton, hoped that it could. And it was toward this end that Mickey had sent the pictures over for Laura's consideration. Any quick glance around her office would confirm that she was well qualified. There were three framed degrees on one of the walls—a medical degree from a prestigious university, another one in psychiatry, and an impressive certificate stating that Dr. Laura Spencer was "Certified by the American Board of Clinical Psychiatrists."

When her secretary buzzed to tell her that Mr. Horton was on the phone, Laura instructed her to say that she was in session and would get back to him. Then she leaned back in her swivel chair and shrugged helplessly. She couldn't keep avoiding Mickey forever. Although they had spoken on the phone several times, they had never met. But even his voice sounded like Bill's. Memories flooded back, unbidden, each one crystal clear. How well she remembered the times her secretary used to tell her "Doctor Horton" was on the phone . . . How often they had planned a joint practice—Spencer & Horton (Bill had often teased about her wish to retain her name when they married). But Bill Horton had left her with no choice. Spencer she was, and Spencer she would now remain.

The same day Laura was looking at the photographs of David and Susan, Mickey Horton sat in the visitors' room of the Salem County jail waiting impatiently for Susan to be brought in from her cell. As he waited, he pulled out a long yellow legal pad and some sharpened pencils and checked through a pile of legal briefs. He had taken on Susan's case reluctantly, only because she was a friend of the family. Mickey was an attractive, bright, up-and-coming lawyer who more usually had successful businessmen and corporations vying for his services.

A guard approached, his hands planted firmly on Susan's shoulders. "She wasn't that interested in coming, Mr. Horton, but I kind of convinced her. Will you be all right alone in here with her, or do you want that I should wait?"

Mickey thanked the guard courteously and dismissed him. He'd practically haunted the courthouse and penal facilities in the early days of his practice when he'd just gotten out of law school, and now he was flattered the staff still remembered him. He allowed Susan to stand in front of him while he pretended to scribble some notes, just to see how she would take it. The young woman who had so recently pumped her husband full of bullets now seemed quiet enough. Out of the corner of his eye, Mickey saw her sullen, stubborn expression, her unkempt hair, her studied air of indifference. She reminded him of a truant standing in a principal's office, waiting for the speech to end so that she could be out and about her mischief once again. Not the ideal client to defend on a murder rap, he thought.

Mickey collected his papers and slid them into his briefcase. Then he stood up and invited Susan to sit down beside him. She shook her head, indicating that she preferred to stand. Mickey sat down again and said, "I don't feel like standing. If we're going to work together at all, I would like to speak to you at eye level. Now sit down and let's get to work. I've wasted enough time as it is waiting for you."

"I had nothing to do with that. *I* didn't ask for you," Susan answered belligerently.

"No. Your mother did. But hear me out. The law insists that you be represented, regardless of how you plead. If it isn't me, it'll be someone who hangs around the court looking for any case, just to pick up a few dollars. Those lawyers are either straight out of law school or over the hill. It really doesn't matter to me. I'm seeing you this once as a favor to your mother. But before I come back again, you're going to have to ask me—very politely—to help you. Then, I may consider it."

Mickey locked his attaché case and stood up to leave. When he was almost at the door, he heard loud, wailing sobs that made him think of a wild animal caught in a steel trap. He turned around and sat down again.

Susan slumped down across from him. "He killed my baby," she cried, repeating it over and over.

Mickey patted her awkwardly on the back and handed her his starched white handkerchief.

"The baby's dead. I'll never see my baby again," she moaned between sniffles.

"I know. That's why I'm here. Now take a deep breath, calm down, and let me help you," Mickey said. Once again he pulled out his yellow legal pad and pencil, poised to take notes.

When Susan Martin was led back to her cell, she pushed aside the movie magazines that littered her cot and sat down. Staring blankly at the wall, she tried to make sense of everything Mickey had said to her. Somehow he'd managed to break through her stubborn resistance. Susan now knew that without the help of Mickey Horton and Dr. Laura Spencer, she would never escape a murder charge. That gave her a lot to think about—that and a dead husband and dead baby. She unfolded Mickey's handkerchief, looked at the initials, and then thought of her own. How often she had doodled the initials S.H.M.—Susan Hunter Martin. Mrs. David Martin.

The young woman who *should have* become Mrs. David Martin was only now beginning to recover from a shattering emotional ordeal. Julie Olson had been David's first and only true love, and everyone had known it. Had Julie not gone out of town one particular weekend to visit her uncle Bill, none of this would have happened. She realized, in retrospect, that her absence had paved the way for Susan Hunter to trick David—first plying him with wine, and then seducing him. From that one fateful encounter, the baby had been conceived. With responsible consideration, Julie had urged David to marry Susan, but only long enough to give the baby his name. Susan had agreed to the proposal to do this and had pledged to release David immediately after the baby's birth so that he could marry Julie—but Susan had not honored the agreement.

In the end, of course, Susan *had* let him go. She'd shot him down with her father's shotgun until he bled to death on her mother's Oriental rug.

Now Julie was learning that the only way to cope with her anguish was to think of others. The only way to bear the death of a loved one was to go on living and help others to do the same. With her aunt Marie's encouragement, she was spending much of her time as a candy striper, visiting the youngest patients at The Willows and helping them learn to walk again or to get around without the use of their legs. Seeing the glee in the faces of young children as she read to them, or made up tales and let them act out the stories, helped her to find some measure of peace.

Julie had first discovered The Willows when Marie's great love, Tony, had been convalescing there and she'd accompanied Marie on visits. When Tony had been discharged as an outpatient, he and Marie had taken a little cottage together. Their strength and courage in coping with his cancer inspired Julie to strive for a similar kind of excellence. They'd shown compassion for Julie and made her feel worthwhile when she had been most vulnerable. Tony's radiance in the midst of pain and Marie's serenity in the face of an uncertain future were models of character and courage for the impressionable young girl.

On his way back from the jail Mickey pondered over his visit to Susan. Then his thoughts turned to Laura and the unreturned phone calls. She's probably soured on the entire Horton family because of Bill, he suspected. Frankly, Mickey couldn't blame her. Mickey's brother Bill had been engaged to

Laura when Mickey had first heard her name. In fact, Bill had raved about her brilliance as a psychiatrist to such an extent that when Diane Hunter had asked Mickey to recommend someone to help her troubled daughter, he had immediately suggested Laura.

But much had changed by then. Bill, who had become a leading surgeon in just a few years after completing his training, had injured his hand in a freak accident. He had received the best of care, but the nerve had been too damaged for a complete recovery. Almost every other field of medicine was still open to him, but the hand that could write prescriptions, use a stethoscope, and perform simple functions could never again hold a scalpel. And Bill's identity had been centered on his self-image as a star surgeon—an innovator, a medical pioneer, and miracle worker. Without being this, his life lost its meaning. Bitterly he'd turned his back on everything, sold his practice, and fled to the West Coast.

"Let Bill find himself," Tom Horton had said to the rest of the family, speaking as a wise father. The family had been understandably hurt and bewildered by his actions, but they loved him and had tried to understand.

In Laura's case, however, it was a different story—she had been his fiancée and he'd left without even saying good-bye.

Laura Spencer's secretary and Mickey Horton's secretary finally managed to set up an appointment for their employers to meet. The secretaries had felt like UN diplomats trying unsuccessfully to arrange a summit meeting. They had become so frustrated by the ongoing game of cat and mouse that they'd secretly placed bets on how long it would take to bring the two "world powers" together.

The meeting finally took place at Salem's most elegant French restaurant. Mickey had chosen it because he felt safe there from other lawyers, reporters, or courthouse hangers-on. However, instead of asking for his favorite table, he secured one on a high, out-of-the-way banquette where they would have maximum privacy.

Laura arrived a few minutes late, spoke with the maître d', and was ceremoniously led to Mickey's table. Although she had never seen Mickey Horton, she would have recognized him anywhere. His eyes were bright with laughter unlike his brother's which smoldered intensely, but both were the Horton family's shade of hazel. When he stood up as she approached, she could see that he was shorter and slimmer than Bill. But the jawline, the way he carried himself, and his self-assurance and warmth were undeniably similar. Laura remembered hearing that there was a third brother, and she wondered fleetingly if all the Hortons resembled one another so strongly.

When introductions had been made and the waiter had taken their order, the two settled back for a long discussion.

"How long was Susan Martin your patient?" David asked.

Laura didn't even have to consult to her notes. "For three sessions."

"That's not possible! Diane told me that she gave Susan checks to cover close to a dozen sessions. She was trying to teach Susan responsibility by having her deposit money into her own account and pay you directly."

"It's an interesting theory," Laura observed wryly, "but it didn't quite work out that way in practice. It merely provided Susan with another source of spending money."

"Damn," Mickey muttered. "Here I had hoped we'd be able to build a solid defense on a whole string of psychiatric sessions."

Even the way Mickey spoke and gestured reminded Laura of Bill. Her mind wandered for a moment as she wondered how many hearts Mickey had broken lately. Would he leave a fiancée and just take off without an explanation because he couldn't practice law? That's not a valid assumption, she corrected herself sternly. Bill Horton would never again be the brilliant surgeon he once was, but he could still practice *medicine*. If for some reason she would no longer be able to practice psychiatry, Laura assured herself, she'd be able to find an acceptable alternative within the medical community.

"Now, with only three sessions," Mickey was saying, breaking into her thoughts, "there may not be enough material for you to use as a witness in her defense."

Laura snapped back to attention. "Nonsense," she retorted briskly. "I've testified in sanity cases, cases of impaired reasoning, custody cases, and others where I interviewed those in question for only one session—and in some cases, that session was shorter than any of the three I had with Susan."

Her certainty delighted Mickey. What a witness! he thought. He leaned forward, smiling, and said, "Now you're talking! With you in our corner, maybe we can save that poor, misguided girl."

"Well," Laura began, "the general focus of my work with Susan was to release her from her negative feelings—her anger, frustration, low self-esteem. She has no *identity* of her own; everything was centered on the baby. *Motherhood* was her career, the only thing she was proud of." Laura paused and avoided Mickey's eyes as she added softly, "It's much the same with a career man who is all wrapped up in a specific profession. If . . . if anything happens to take that away from him, something snaps."

The message came through loud and clear. For a moment Laura looked up to meet Mickey's eyes and was held there by the words unspoken between them. But this was neither the time nor the place to discuss Bill Horton—and they knew it. Turning away from him, Laura continued her analysis of Susan's emotional stability. "When her father rejected her, it only increased her negative self-image. There again, it was all or nothing. Her mother may have loved her, but that didn't count. David didn't love Susan, but she thought she could force him to, through sheer willpower. Well, it hadn't worked with her father and it certainly wasn't going to work with David, who probably loved Julie until the day he died."

Mickey nodded in agreement.

"Then there was the baby," Laura continued.

"I get you!" Mickey said enthusiastically, suddenly realizing where Laura was heading. "The baby was the only human being whose love Susan felt sure of. Once the baby was killed, she cracked. David was the bringer of bad tidings—it's like the king killing the messenger who brings the bad news." He reached across the table to touch her in order to communicate his excitement. Laura smiled and then pulled back: she had learned to be wary of Horton men.

"There was more to it than that," she reminded him.

"If there was, then the city is to blame. When David Martin sat on a swing in a public park and placed his son on his lap, he was merely doing what he had done several times before. The baby had always been secure and safe in his father's lap, swinging back and forth. This time, though, the rusty chain snapped. David did his best to shield the infant, suffering multiple bruises in the process. He hadn't even realized that his wrist was broken when he went along with Officer Klein to tell Susan what had happened. The break in the bone only came out in the autopsy."

Laura nodded knowingly. "A posttrauma effect. I've seen it happen many times before. People get so emotionally devastated that they don't realize what injuries they've sustained. Sometimes they're completely unaware of what they're doing."

Mickey's eyes glowed with barely suppressed excitement.

"Doctor, you have just spelled out my defense of Susan. A highly excitable, neurotic young woman, still in her teens, hears from her husband that her infant was just killed while in his care, and . . . boom! Off goes the shotgun."

Laura nodded and made some notes to herself. "That much is true. But there must be more to the defense than that. There always *has been* whenever I was called upon to testify in court."

"Of course there's more," said Mickey. "You're perfectly right. We'll have to develop a formidable defense, or that youngster will lose her freedom, possibly for the rest of her life."

Laura felt herself stiffen when Mickey said "we." Sitting face to face with the image of Bill Horton was difficult enough. Working so closely together with him would be something else again. She wasn't sure that she'd be able to control her emotions.

Mickey must have sensed her ambivalence, because he smiled encouragingly and extended his hand to her as a sign of peace.

After a moment's hesitation, Laura reached out and clasped it warmly.

"Don't think I'm unaware of all that you've been through," Mickey said gently. "The whole family has heard so many wonderful things about you from Bill that we're all eager to meet you. Under happier circumstances, of course."

Laura said nothing and merely studied her plate.

"Have you heard where Bill is?" he asked quietly. Laura shook her head. "We got word through a mutual friend only yesterday."

"Last thing I heard, he flew to California."

"That much we knew," Mickey concurred. "They've got a huge clinic out there for Korean War veterans. Some of them have been out there for years, trying to put their lives together. A friend of my father's is there overseeing the medical team, and he recognized Bill at once. Bill just showed up one day and volunteered to work with the Red Cross. He never told another living soul."

"So he didn't even have the decency to inform his own family where he was going," Laura said bitterly.

Mickey hesitated, trying to find the words to make her understand. "I know what he's put you through, Laura. But think how lucky you are to be able to lose yourself in your work. Bill desperately needs something like that right now. In a way, both of us are lucky, to be useful and needed in the helping professions we've chosen for ourselves.

Between the two of us, maybe we can help Susan."

"You're right, of course," Laura replied after a moment. "How much better it is to fight for your beliefs than to cut and run. The Red Cross's gain may have been my loss, but right now I'm tired of losing. Maybe between the two of us we can win this case."

Mickey signaled the waiter to pour the wine. Then he and Laura clicked glasses. This time, please let me keep it platonic, Laura thought. If Mickey was thinking anything else, he kept it even from himself.

Susan Martin, led into court by a matron and two guards, was wearing that same sullen expression Mickey had seen on her face the first time he'd visited her in jail. Evidently, the pep talks he and Laura had given her hadn't been able to work miracles in such a short period of time. At least her mother had come through. Diane Hunter had selected the perfect outfit for her daughter: neither too flashy nor too somber. Mickey had specifically asked Diane to pick something youthful, something that would remind both the judge and jury that this was a girl with her whole life ahead of her.

When everyone had been seated, the clerk asked all to rise for the entrance of the judge.

Judge Collins had been a tennis champ in college and frequently played opposite Mickey in doubles matches at the club. He was always relaxed and easy, quick to kid the other players about their backhand.

Now, though, thinking about the case before him, he was somber. Clearly this was a case that troubled him.

And it was a troubling case all right—to the judge, the prosecuting district attorney . . . and especially to Mickey. When he had asked for bail at the arraignment, he'd been turned down. And, as he'd expected, all attempts to have the case dropped had been denied. An assault had been committed with a dangerous weapon and the victim had died as a result. The act had been unpremeditated, so murder in the first degree was ruled out. But any homicide with a loaded weapon brought a mandatory charge of murder in the second degree.

The case had been all over the local papers and television news shows and had even been picked up by the wire services. The "Rock-a-bye Baby Case," as it had been coined by the media, had already gained a great deal of notoriety. The famous nursery song seemed particularly apt to newspaper editors: "When the bough breaks, the cradle will fall, Down will come baby, cradle and all." Editorial cartoonists had picked up the idea and used it. One of them showed a chilling drawing of a Superwoman type resembling Susan, with wild hair shooting out in all directions like thunderbolts and a huge blunderbuss in her hands. She stood with a look of triumph on her face as smoke curled up from the gun. One foot was planted firmly on the floor, the other on the chest of her prey—David Martin.

Earlier, Mickey had asked for a change of venue, arguing that the defense could not expect an impartial hearing in this locality. Judge Collins had sat him down and said, "Look, Counselor. The entire state has heard of this case. That cartoon has crossed state lines, and negotiations are already in progress with the newspaper and artist to turn it into a poster. I doubt if you'd be able to find a jury within hundreds of miles who won't already have formed *some* kind of opinion about it."

"All the more reason to—"

"Please let me finish, Counselor. I suggest that we try the case right here. If you can fault the results on the basis of prejudice on the part of the jury, you'll have an opportunity to have the verdict thrown out by a higher court."

"You say that is what you *suggest*?" asked Mickey.

"Yes."

"What if I put it to you as a motion to change venue?"

The judge folded his hands in front of him and stared at Mickey. "Then I would have to say motion denied."

It was indeed a setback, and Mickey said so afterward to Laura.

"Is there any way I can help?" she asked sympathetically.

Mickey sighed with relief and answered, "I was hoping you would ask. It's a request that I didn't want to burden you with, but..."

"Here it comes." Laura smiled. "I put my

foot in it, didn't I? What is that old army saying—'Never volunteer'?"

As Mickey warmly returned her smile, Laura reflected that since they'd started working together on the case, they'd gotten to know each other better. She realized now that in many ways, Mickey was nothing like Bill. Mickey was calm, almost serene in the face of adversity; he was also *dependable* and a steadying influence on all those around him. She listened as he explained to her how crucial it was that they get an open-minded, if not sympathetic, jury.

"If you could sit near the witness table and look each potential juror straight in the eye, you might be able to spot the slight hesitations, the evasive eyes, the general facial expressions and body language."

"Who does this for you when I'm not around?" Laura teased in a slightly flirtatious manner.

Mickey began to reply seriously, then caught her undertone and said, "Certainly no one with your perception, professional acumen, and stunning style. You know, you're going to spoil me, Laura."

And that might not be a bad thing, Laura thought to herself. She was beginning to realize how much responsibility Mickey carried on those broad shoulders. He was a friend, an adviser—and, for most of his family and all of his friends, a shoulder to lean on. Her training had taught her that such a burden could prove a strain and should be relieved from time to time—or at least modified. The same training also prevented her from giving unsolicited advice.

With Laura's help, Mickey was able to agree with the DA on a jury after three days. He was more than satisfied with his selection, neither regretting any particular juror nor feeling as if he'd had to compromise. Laura had rearranged her patient schedule so that she could watch as Mickey interviewed prospective jurors, alert for any elusive nuances of prejudice or partiality.

"Hey, we make quite a team, the two of us," Mickey commented to Laura as they grabbed a quick cup of coffee after the last juror had been selected. He said it with such open, boyish enthusiasm that she could have hugged him. But she stopped herself in time. Too quickly, she cautioned herself. This relationship is happening too quickly. She flashed him an impersonal smile and said, "Let's see if it's a *winning* team, Counselor. Don't forget, the trial is still ahead of us."

In the past few weeks, Susan had become all too familiar with the mind-numbing, unrelenting monotony of prison life—one day dragging slowly, predictably into the next, with nothing to relieve the utter boredom. Now, in the courtroom, she felt like a kid in a candy store. Letting her eyes wander, she pretended that *she* was the judge.

How powerful he must feel, she thought, sitting so high above us, like some kind of god. The jury looked like bowling pins lined up in a row. The court clerk administered the docket, the stenotypist's hands were poised on the keys of the special typewriter, the DA and his assistants sat on one side, and Mickey and Laura waited for her on the other. The first few rows behind them were filled with friends and relatives and newspaper reporters.

Suddenly it hit her that everyone—but *everyone*—in the courtroom was here because of *her*. It was awesome. *She was the center* of all this attention. For a moment she struggled to suppress an irreverent giggle. If only her father could see her. Or Julie. She was glad now that her mother had made her dress with care.

Out of the corner of his eye, Mickey saw a wicked grin flicker across Susan's face and decided that he much preferred her sullen expression. He was relieved that he and Laura had both agreed Susan should not be called in her own defense. They'd found in their interviews with her that the rage and stubbornness she manifested was frightening to behold. The jury would surely be unfavorably influenced by her as soon as she opened her mouth. Again and again they'd instructed her to "look interested and attentive, but to remain quiet." If she had anything to say, they'd told her, she should make notes and wait until recess to discuss whatever was on her mind. He hoped she remembered—and would obey.

The case itself was clear-cut. Under questioning, Officer Klein recalled how he was first called to the scene of the accident—the playground in the park where the swing had broken and the baby had died. He continued to the point where he'd offered to go inside with David and support the young man emotionally as he broke the news to his wife about the accidental death of their son.

"I could kick myself, sir, every time I think how I should have insisted that I accompany him in. But he seemed so definite, so convinced that he could handle it alone. I have four children of my own, and I know that something like that could have driven me crazy too."

This last sentence had been offered in reply to Mickey's cross-examination, and it made DA Rice cringe. It supported the very argument of Mickey's case—temporary insanity.

Carefully, Mickey led Klein through the rest of his testimony—how he had heard loud gunshot blasts and rushed into the apartment. The description of Susan blasting away at her downed, bleeding husband and then screaming, sounded so much like the now famous editorial cartoon that Mickey wondered if the cartoonist had interviewed Klein.

After Klein was dismissed, Mickey addressed the court. "The defense wishes to make it clear, Your Honor, that we do not deny Susan Martin's finger was on the trigger, that she held the gun when it went off, killing her husband. We merely contend that the act was unpremeditated. That in all likelihood, she hadn't the least idea what she was doing. That in Officer's Klein's own words, describing how he might have felt in Susan's stead, she went crazy."

When the district attorney objected sternly, reminding the court that *loading* a gun constituted premeditation, Mickey was quick to reply, "I have before me, Your Honor, a sworn deposition from the defendant's father, who couldn't be in court with us today, blaming his own carelessness for that. Both the shotgun and long rifle were stored away loaded. The man was so careless that I am amazed his fishing poles were not armed with hook and lure. Out of his entire 'sportsman's' arsenal, the only unloaded items were two seventeenth-century dueling pistols. I assume that was because antique cartridges were not available."

At the judge's instruction, the deposition was placed in evidence. Mickey hardly needed to emphasize that a traumatized young woman might easily pick up the closest thing at hand without realizing what she was doing.

Diane Hunter took the stand next and testified that she had been after Susan for weeks to go through her father's personal belongings and help herself to whatever she wanted. When Sam Hunter left for New York, he not only divorced his wife, but his daughter, friends, and former possessions as well.

"When Sam used to come home from a day of tennis or golf," Diane Hunter recalled, her eyes filling with tears, "he would step out of his sweaty clothes and leave them in a heap for me to pick up. It was always up to someone else to take care of his messes. When he stepped out of the marriage, it was the same thing. He stepped out of one life and into another. And what a mess of broken lives he left behind." With that, Diane broke down and cried.

The district attorney watched as Mickey comforted the defendant's mother. Then he saw members of the jury lean forward solicitously. No, he decided, I won't gain anything by cross-examining a poor, distraught woman.

The defense's final witness was Dr. Laura Spencer. Mickey insisted that she give, when asked, the entire string of her impressive credentials. He had her mention the various articles she had written for prestigious psychiatric and medical journals. The testimony itself was masterful. She and Mickey had gone over it so many times that it just rolled out, clearly and concisely. Mickey then turned to DA Rice with a gesture that invited him to do his best. Giving Laura's hand a reassuring pat, he leaned over and whispered to her, "Remember, it's less important what you say than how you say it. He's going to try to bait you. Whatever you do, please don't lose your cool."

Rice took a deep, calming breath. This

was his last chance to discredit the case for the defense. Mickey had skillfully argued that if his client had lost her mind during the commission of a felony, she could not possibly have known right from wrong at the given moment—hence the term "temporary insanity." Rice reflected that he would have loved to put Susan on the stand and grill her unmercifully, but he knew Mickey had wisely chosen to keep the sullen, resentful young woman off the stand. Resolutely, he approached Laura Spencer.

Laura smiled pleasantly at Rice, noticing how tense he was. She could see a little vein throb in his temple as he clenched and unclenched his fist. Mickey had told her that Rice was too ambitious for his own good. He fancied himself as a crusader of justice and was using the DA's office as a stepping-stone to higher political office.

The questions flew thick and fast. The louder *he* spoke, the softer Laura spoke. The faster he snapped out questions, the slower and more considered were her answers. None of this lost the jury. When he finally questioned her qualifications for defining and recognizing temporary insanity, she surprised even Mickey with her answer. Pulling a card out of her pocket, she glanced at it before speaking.

"I had forgotten about this until my secretary brought it to my attention this morning," she said. "Here are a few citations from the *American Journal of Legal Jurisprudence* and from our own state bar journal."

"I don't need the help of law journals at this stage of my career, thank you," Rice said officiously. "I am quite capable of defining legal insanity without any help."

The judge looked at Mickey and asked if he wanted to enter the list as evidence. Mickey caught the slightest affirmative nod from Laura and replied, "Yes, Your Honor."

Then the judge looked down at Laura and asked, "Once we read these citations, Dr. Spencer, what will we have learned that is pertinent to this case?"

Laura smiled easily and said, "I believe that Mr. Rice had been questioning my qualifications. I thought it might help to show the various legal bodies, including state supreme courts, that have quoted me extensively as an authority. I didn't have time to go over this with counsel, Your Honor, so I apologize if I have spoken out of turn."

The clerk handed the judge Laura's citations. He looked at the long list before him, marveling at how such an attractive young woman could be so advanced in her field. Then he looked at Laura and saw what the jury saw—her innate modest courtesy. Here would be a nice young woman to sit down and chat with, to confide in, to bring one's problems to.

"Most impressive," said Judge Collins, "most impressive indeed. Here you are, Counselor." Reluctantly, Rice walked over and glanced quickly at the list, frowning with annoyance as he read. The jury craned their necks to get a peek, and Judge Collins announced, "All of this will be entered in the record, available for you to examine for as long as you wish."

They sat back, satisfied. Soon afterward, when Laura was dismissed from the stand, the eyes of the jury followed her. She smiled at them unselfconsciously, and they couldn't help but smile too.

Not surprisingly, the jury came back after only three hours to pronounce the verdict: not guilty by virtue of temporary insanity.

Mickey swept Laura up in his arms. He accepted congratulations from colleagues and friends, shook hands with Susan, and kissed Diane on the cheek. Then, with Laura in tow, he raced out of the courtroom to celebrate.

Over a fancy dinner that evening, Mickey couldn't take his eyes off Laura. She basked in his attention, feeling that it was wonderful to have a normal, decent, outgoing, generous man in love with her—it was such a contrast to what she had so recently been through! Between bites of a succulent crown roast, Mickey reeled off all the family members he wanted Laura to meet.

Neither of them could have guessed how soon she would meet them all, and under what sad circumstances. Almost an hour later, as they were having after-dinner brandy and crepes suzette, Mickey's secretary, Carla, tracked him down to tell him that Tony Merritt had just died in his sleep.

She explained that Julie was staying over at Marie's for the night, and the family had asked Mickey's help in making funeral arrangements.

"This is so, so sad," Mickey said in a subdued voice to Laura. "Tony was one of the finest men you'd ever want to meet. My heart goes out to Marie. She's been through so much."

Laura, whose heart went out to Mickey, could understand.

Chapter Two

The Gift of Love

Laura met the Horton clan under quiet, saddened circumstances. Although everyone was gracious, all were understandably concerned about Marie. Mickey had mentioned to Laura that his sister had been severely depressed over the past year, yet she showed no overt signs of it now. If anything, Marie seemed to be comforting her family as much as they were comforting her.

Between the celebration dinner following the trial and the day of the funeral, Mickey had proposed and Laura had accepted. The couple decided to get married simply and privately. Neither of them thought it fitting to have a fancy wedding so soon after a funeral. Besides, they were so caught up in each other that all they really wanted was to be alone.

Once again, their two secretaries were actively helpful in setting up an "appointment" for them—this time for their elopement. Like two children let out of school before a holiday, Mickey and Laura joyously departed, eager to make up for lost time. Mickey was tired of being referred to as "that eligible bachelor," and Laura was determined to make up for all the disappointments she'd experienced with Bill. On their wedding night the newlyweds both decided to start a family immediately. They loved babies and envisioned a household crowded with happy children. Between them, it seemed, there was more than enough love and joy to fill the whole world.

To their amazement, they discovered they had more in common than they'd ever dreamed could be shared by two people in love. Both of them were romantic, even though they tried to hide it from other people. Each had the gift of great understanding of others. And they realized they could mutually nurture this both between themselves and toward the people they came into contact with in their jobs—Mickey's clients and Laura's patients. Both had the ability to look beyond words into the real meaning of things and to sense and share emotions. Laura and Mickey recited poetry to each other and had a repertoire of private jokes that always prompted smiles, conspiratorial winks, or bursts of spontaneous laughter.

"Wow!" Mickey exclaimed happily. "I feel just like a kid again."

"*Again*?" Laura teased. "I'd say for the first time. You probably acted like a little grown-up when you were still in grade school."

"You're right, you know," Mickey agreed after a moment's reflection. "Tommy was always the cut-up, the class clown, the popular, crazy funnyman. And Bill brooded a lot, practicing to be famous and impressive. And I pretended to be grown-up as soon as I could tie my own sneakers."

"I thought so," remarked Laura as she kissed him on the nose. "Tell me about Tommy. I know more than I want to about Bill."

"By now I guess I can conclude that he was probably killed in Korea. He was sent there at the tail end of the Korean War. He kept up a steady spate of letters, then all of a sudden . . . nothing! The family contacted everyone they could think of. One of Dad's classmates at medical school was an assistant surgeon general. We called our senators, congressmen, everybody. He's still technically listed as missing in action. But there're only so many years you can keep hoping. For my mother's sake I still use MIA terminology. But in our hearts, everyone else in the family has given him up for dead."

To break the mood, he picked up a book of romantic poems they had bought earlier that day in a gift shop that carried Victoriana. Each of them picked a stanza to read aloud, and, when there were only a few stanzas left to read, Mickey put down the book and Laura turned out the light. Lovingly, they turned to each other . . . losing themselves in the passion they later declared to be the finest poetry of all—the poetry of two bodies inextricably entwined.

Mickey's niece, Julie Olson, had never felt so absolutely alone in her life. When David died, Marie and Tony took her to their hearts, often urging her to stay overnight with them in their cottage. The deep love this couple shared provided a perfect atmosphere to ease her pain as she grieved for her slain lover. Then Tony had died. Once his cancer had spread to his bone marrow, every realized that he had little time left. Still, the reality of his death had taken Julie by surprise.

There was no Tony to talk to, no Marie to cry with — Marie had enough of a challenge putting the pieces of her own life together. How could Julie possibly go to her so soon after the funeral and say, "What can I do? I'm pregnant."

There was no question in her mind that it was David's child. When the two of them had met to talk, miserable and frustrated by Susan's refusal to divorce David, they had spent one long, passionate day together. Until that day Julie had been a virgin, and after that day she had been chaste. She was certain she could never again love another man as she had loved David. And without such a love, any physical relationship was unthinkable.

She thought of her uncle Mickey — she had gone to him when Susan had announced she was carrying David's baby — but Mickey was on his honeymoon and Marie was in mourning, so Julie let the days slip by, wondering what she was going to do. At one point she thought she might confide in her grandparents. Then she remembered all they had been through in the past couple of years and decided not to say anything to them. Julie had always been slender and athletic. Although they saw her every day, it would be quite a while before they'd notice any difference in her figure. In a couple of months she could wear looser clothing and nobody would be able to tell a thing. But sooner or later she'd have to do something. She was grateful for one thing—her parents were separated from her by a large body of water, the Atlantic Ocean. She wanted to be millions of miles away the day that Ben Olson learned that the apple of his eye, his only daughter, was carrying an illegitimate baby. All hell would break loose then.

Julie went to the library and took out books about pregnancy and child care. The more she read, the more concerned she became. All the books advised starting to see a doctor during the early months of pregnancy and following a preparatory regimen with a good diet, exercise, and careful monitoring of the body.

In the end, she told no one. She made sure that her school attendance records were perfect. She concentrated on her studies and watched her marks improve. She crossed her fingers a lot. She thought that maybe, if she were a model student and human being, she would be rewarded with the perfect solution to what had become an almost insurmountable problem.

Deep down in her heart, however, she was afraid that none of her efforts would mean a thing. She cried for her dead David and lost weight worrying.

"Your appointment has arrived, Mrs. Barnes," the secretary announced over the intercom. Marcy Barnes picked up her phone and instructed the secretary to have him wait. Then she glanced at the memo once more, still puzzled by its contents. Dr. William Horton was requesting permission to continue his work with one of the patients far away from the Red Cross facilities here in San Diego. On a day like today—a near perfect day, like many days there—Marcy couldn't understand this. San Diego had a good climate so Marcy reasoned the weather was not an issue. And Dr. Horton had not specified a time for his return, which made the request itself even more irregular.

The patient in question was Mark Brooks. Once again, Marcy reviewed his folder. Brooks had evidently been one of the sadder casualties of the Korean War. Captured years before by the North Koreans and tortured extensively, he had been a broken man when the Red Cross had first discovered him. Some of the damage done to him might well be permanent. The torturing he had gone through would have been enough to drive any man insane. Plus it was later discovered that the isolation cage in which he had been found had been his home for months, if not for years.

Marcy chided herself for taking each case so personally. After all this time as a chief administrator, she should have been able to keep from filling up with tears. But Brooks was a case, a person, who brought tears. He had lost his memory and, with it, his name. His face had been so battered and burned that he needed extensive plastic surgery. If he'd ever had a family, their was no way of finding it now. With neither face nor name, he was completely alone in the world.

Not completely, though, she corrected herself. Dr. William Horton was waiting right now in her outside office, evidently willing—even eager—to take responsibility for the unfortunate young man.

Marcy replaced the folders on her desk, picked up her purse, and went into the adjoining washroom. There she fixed each curl on her head and sprayed it. Then she touched up her mascara, and applied fresh lipstick. Bill Horton was the handsomest man she had ever seen outside of the movies. With smooth, sun-streaked blond hair and huge hazel eyes, he could make any woman fall in love with him, even if he were just been a failure. But he was also a successful doctor who had left his practice under tragic circumstances to come out to California as a volunteer worker for the Red Cross. The combination was irresistible.

There were all sorts of rumors and speculations as to the nature of his "tragedy"—

everything from a broken heart to a broken home. But Marcy was content not to conjecture and to accept him as he was. He was great to look at and extremely competent at everything he did.

She signaled her secretary to send him in.

"Hello, Bill," she said, smiling at him. "I'm probably speaking for everyone else at this facility when I say how sorry I am to see you go. To have a doctor full-time, day and night, on the premises has spoiled us. And one who refuses to take a cent of . . ."

Bill waved away the mention of money. "I did pretty well at my private practice and will be able to once again," he said firmly.

"Is that where you'll be going now?"

"Same state, but a different hospital. I used to divide my practice between the Upstate Medical Hospital and Salem General Hospital. Salem is my hometown, and I think I'll concentrate my work right there from now on."

Marcy couldn't take her eyes off him. If I were only fifteen or twenty years younger, she thought. She couldn't help asking if he had a wife and children.

"Family, yes, in the way of brothers and sisters and parents. But I haven't married . . . yet. I had to leave a fiancée at home when I flew out here. I only hope that she forgives me for taking time out of our lives for a while."

Marcy wanted to tell him that *she* could forgive him *anything*, but she bit her tongue and picked up his memo instead, running her eyes over it in a businesslike manner. "What's this about Mark Brooks?"

"The only reason he's living here at the facility is because he's homeless and not completely able to cope with the outside world. We gave him his name, and before long, we'll be able to give him a new face. I'd like to supervise the process. There will be more extensive skin grafts and bone grafts over a period of time. Since I have a background in surgery, I'll have access to the finest board-certified plastic surgeons or, at least, to a better choice than would be available to the general practitioners who visit here twice a week."

Bill paused a moment, trying to phrase his next comment. "Besides, I never had to fight in a war and suffer like these poor devils. If I can help salvage this one life, I'll figure that I have made some small contribution."

"How does Mark feel about it?" Marcy asked softly.

"I've told him about leaving, and he seemed interested in details about my hometown. When I told him he might visit, he seemed excited at the prospect. But I didn't want to say more until I got the go-ahead from you."

The go-ahead was given. Mark was invited and responded with bewildered gratitude. The entire staff could see that he would need someone to lean on for a while before he could ever make his way alone in the world. How lucky he was, they agreed, that someone like Dr. Horton took such an interest in him.

When Bill Horton arrived home with Mark Brooks in tow, the first call he made was to Laura's office. There was a touch of triumph in the secretary's voice when she told him that Laura was out of town. She almost crowed the answer to his second question, "On her honeymoon, with Mickey Horton." The secretary had endured so much with her boss when Doctor Bill had deserted her that this was a moment she'd been dreaming of.

It was the second blow to Bill's ego within the course of a year. If he hadn't taken responsibility for Mark Brooks and brought him along, he would surely have packed his belongings and left town once again.

Bill had been programmed for success. All through childhood he had worshiped his father's profession and been encouraged in the direction of science and medicine. In medical school he had taken easily to the triumphs of surgery. Being the star member of a surgical team, performing for a gallery of colleagues while others waited anxiously outside or crowded around monitors to watch every flick of the scapel—this, to Bill, had been heaven.

When he hung up the phone, the realization that he'd lost both his career and the love of his life almost destroyed him. He could blame fate for the nerve disorder that had disabled his hand; he could blame no one but himself for the loss of Laura.

If only *he* could fall out of love as quickly as she had . . . Suddenly he was struck by a startling thought. Perhaps she'd married Mickey on the rebound! After a quick reflection, he felt he had to be right. A love like they had could never be destroyed so easily—simply by one person's running away from it. Neither his trip to California nor Laura's honeymoon meant a thing. He felt if he bided his time until she returned, he'd be able to see her, and talk with her. And he was sure that after just a few minutes alone, he'd know if their love were truly dead. It just didn't seem possible.

Whenever she could, Julie dropped over to visit Marie. Although she would never burden her aunt with her own problem, she nevertheless found Marie a source of solace. She talked about David, and Marie reminisced about Tony.

"Of course he's still a part of me," Marie was saying, "just as David will always be a part of you. The difference is that Tony and I both knew when he was dying, and we could prepare ourselves—prepare not only for death, but for life, for enjoying every moment left to its fullest."

"But the two of you were together. With David and me, Susan stood between us. Then she . . . she . . . killed him."

Marie put her arm around Julie and said gently, "I know, dear, but we must go on. Each of us must find our own way. You are on this planet for a certain amount of time. You've got to take the responsibility for your life, because nobody else will."

Not daring to mention her pregnancy, Julie asked Marie whom she used to go to with her problems when she was Julie's age.

"My mother, I suppose," Marie answered. "But now I'm living my own life and making my own choices."

When Tony died, Tom and Alice had opened their home to their daughter, eager to comfort her in whatever way they could. Marie had thanked them but declined, preferring to remain in the tiny cottage where she and Tony had spent their last months together. He had left her the money he'd inherited from his mother, and that was more than enough to pay her monthly expenses.

"Guess who's coming over later?" Marie said cheerfully. "Your uncle Bill, back from California at last. He suffered a terrible blow and worked his way out of it by caring for sick and wounded veterans. If I were a doctor, that's just what I would do."

But Julie could find no solace in these words. In a little while she would have to care for the tiny being growing inside of her right now. Although it was still too early for her pregnancy to be noticeable, she'd already begun wearing loose clothes.

In one sense, Mark was a godsend. By bringing him along to visit, Bill could drop in on his family and close friends and keep the conversation from growing too personal. He had no desire to discuss the way he felt about having lost his ability as a surgeon—or about having lost Laura.

His first visit was to Marie though Julie had left early, preoccupied with her own concerns. Marie had prepared a light snack and baked a cake for the occasion. Amazed, Bill watched as his sister actually got a smile out of Mark. True, it was a wry smile, but at least it was a beginning.

"I think you were very clever to get to name yourself," she said to him. You had a choice most people don't get. Did you pick Mark Brooks because the names meant something to you—a favorite character in a book or a hero in a movie?"

It had generally been hard to tell through all of Mark's bandages whether he was grimacing or frowning, but now his smile was unmistakable. "I wasn't that clever," he replied. "I let some of the nurses help. I had lots of time for reading, so when they asked me who my favorite author was, I said, 'Mark Twain.' I don't exactly remember where the 'Brooks' comes from."

"You have a brand-new life ahead of you," Marie observed, her eyes twinkling. "You can write like Mark Twain did or babble like a brook. Or even do both at once, if the idea pleases you. You've got an assortment of choices!"

Up to this point Mark had always felt very dismal about his plight. And although he was ashamed of it, he felt very sorry for himself. But now here was this wonderful woman who had only recently suffered a deep, tragic loss and who yet could see the bright side of life. This gave him hope.

Perhaps he too could break through his gloom.

After getting back in touch with close friends and relatives, Bill dropped by Salem General Hospital. He was pleased to be welcomed back on staff and accepted reassignment to the surgery group—in an administrative capacity for the present. After a few months, he was told, he could meet with department heads to discuss where else he thought he might fit in. He was fully qualified in several other areas, for example, to join his father in the practice of internal medicine or Dr. Conrad in the pathology department. Laura was in psychiatry there, and he knew it was just as well that he wasn't qualified to be in that department. Working side by side with Mrs. *Mickey* Horton might prove uncomfortable, to say the least.

Before Bill reported to work, he took a day to introduce Mark Brooks to the surgery department. He had sent all the Xrays, slides, and files ahead to prepare the staff, who concurred with Bill's plans for Mark. It would be a long, slow, tedious job building up a face from a mass of bone, cartilage, and scar tissue. But the young man was strong enough for the doctors to begin making plans for him.

Now the question was, how would Mark spend his days? Bill's spacious apartment had two spare rooms, three bathrooms, and a separate entrance, so he and Mark certainly wouldn't get in each other's way.

But Mark was shy and unused to life outside a hospital. He would probably spend his time reading at home, afraid to show his bandaged face.

Marie came up with the perfect solution. She asked Bill if it might not be a good idea to have Mark drop by for an hour or two in the afternoons. "We could call it memory lessons," she said. "Even though I never completed college, I majored in psychology, and I know something about word association. I could write flash cards with names and places on them, and who knows? Maybe something will jog his memory."

Mark was delighted and couldn't wait to get started. He thought Marie was the most wonderful woman he had ever met.

Chapter Three

Obsession

Ben Olson was living high. As a small-town banker in Salem, he had parlayed a few substantial international accounts and multimillionaire contacts into a worldwide banking empire. Depending upon the business conducted and the clients to be seen, Ben had the use of company suites in Paris, London, and Geneva. His wife, Addie, preferred to have him time his Paris business to coincide with the seasonal fashion shows there, particularly those of the more famous couturiers.

Ben was only too happy to oblige. A well-turned-out, smashing-looking wife had perhaps been the single most important factor in his climb to the top. Somehow Addie knew instinctively which Kuwaiti businessmen, Mexican sugar refiners, and Iranian oil men to smile at, then how to occupy their wives while Ben clinched the deals.

To the international set, they were an ideal couple. Addie couldn't have been any more delighted with her ever-expanding position in life. Sometimes, when the parties were elaborate enough, or the sunsets on the Riviera spectacular enough, or the shipping magnate's yacht awesome enough, she imagined that she was still a schoolgirl, seated in a movie house in Salem, lost in a magical land of make-believe.

As an international banker, Ben had more than his share of problems and stress—but he claimed to thrive on it all. As well as helping to enlarge his bank account, all the sipping and nibbling he did was increasing his waistline and blood pressure. But when his doctor told him to slow down, Ben replied that he had no intention of doing so—he was having the time of his life.

Addie and Ben had enrolled their young son, Stephan, at Eton. But Ben really had only one missing factor that would make his life complete—his daughter, Julie. Each time the Olsons visited the estate of a titled English family, Ben would wistfully ask the young daughter of the house about herself, where she went to school, what she was learning. Then he would take out a photograph of Julie. In answer to questions, he always said that she would be joining them "any time now."

He begrudged every month of Julie's senior year in high school. She had fought long and hard to stay with her grandparents for this last year. He kept asking Addie,

"Who among those in our social set has ever heard of Salem High School? What earthly use is a diploma from a local high school? Why can't she finish in France or Switzerland or England, where she could learn to speak all the important languages and acquire the necessary social skills?"

Addie had to remind him that he was talking to a graduate of the same stateside high school who had arrived in Europe with the same language skills. "I hope you're not ashamed of *me*, honey," she said with a playful smile. But she knew, even before he opened his mouth to reassure her, that in his eyes she was perfect. However, Ben Olson disliked many of his in-laws because of what he considered to be their small-town attitudes. He begrudged their influence on his wife and was delighted that an ocean now separated the Olsons from the Hortons.

Ben counted the days until Julie would be able to join them. Toward that end he had actually compiled a list of "eligible" young men whose fathers were clients or associates of his within the international community. Their nationalities ranged from Chilean to Portuguese, and their family estates often approached the billion-dollar level. He had once shown his list to Addie and asked, "Well, what do you think? Are you prepared to be an in-law?"

If Addie hadn't known Ben and Julie as well as she had, she might have exploded. To her, the idea of choosing one's son-in-law seemed like something out of the Dark Ages.

But if it was good enough for titled royalty and Middle Eastern billionaires, it was good enough for Ben. "Why in the world would they want Julie?" she asked. "What does a small-town girl have to offer an eligible young man from such a family?"

"You leave that up to *me*," Ben retorted. "You've never understood that child as I do. Julie has always been able to achieve whatever has been important to her. With my contacts and encouragement, she won't have any trouble."

That was just the point, Addie thought. Julie might not be the least bit interested in any of the young men her father paraded in front of her. Either way, Ben's ego always led him to overestimate the charm and attractiveness of *his* daughter.

And, sighing, Addie was forced to admit that she might not be reacting so objectively herself. She knew she had a jealous streak, which, when combined with her possessiveness over Ben, often colored *her* judgment. Once, when Julie was still a child, Ben had been showing her how to work a jigsaw puzzle while across the room her mother had been showing family photographs to a friend.

"Oh, what a beautiful picture that is of you, Addie," the friend had exclaimed.

"Yes, it is nice, isn't it, " Addie had agreed complacently. "It's a shame that neither of the children take after me. With a boy, it isn't important, but with a girl . . ."

Later, when Ben had chided her for

speaking in that manner in front of Julie, she'd replied, "Well, it's true, isn't it?" Ben had been about to protest that it was indeed *untrue*. In his eyes, Julie was the most beautiful child he had ever seen. But he'd caught the fire in his wife's eyes and held his tongue. It was crucial, he knew, that everyone confirm Addie's beauty and downplay similar qualities in *any* other female—even a nine-year-old child.

This was what held the Olsons' marriage together. Ben was Addie's mirror, her assurance that she was the fairest in the land. In return, Addie was his rapt audience and his ego builder. She made him feel he was a tiger in bed and a wit at parties. Her bright, tinkling laugh accompanied every joke he told, whether or not she'd heard it countless times before. Early in their marriage, they'd struck another bargain— whatever *private* disagreements they had, they would always agree in public. This would be especially important, they realized, when it came to disciplining the children. Most times they spoke as a single voice. And if they disagreed, Ben's vote usually carried.

A single exception occurred when Ben conceded to Addie's request that Julie be allowed to finish school in Salem. It had been a hard-fought battle, and practically the only time mother and daughter had completely agreed with each other—each for her own reasons.

Addie didn't want an almost grown-up daughter cramping her style. She loved to have younger men flirt with her as if she were a girl their own age. And she welcomed having Ben entirely to herself. Julie was blossoming into an uncomfortably pretty young woman. If Addie saw her every day, she would have to admit as much to herself.

Beneath these mixed emotions and ambiguous motivations, Addie was capable of maternal feelings. They sometimes cropped up under the most surprising circumstances, even on occasions when her fragile ego felt threatened. But she rarely crossed Ben. He wanted his word to be law, and she generally supported him in this.

With the same industry and determination that had secured him a banking empire, Ben now set out to polish up the family name and proudly trot it out for display. He had hired a scholar from the Royal College of Genealogy to chart the recorded history and line of descent for both the Olson and Horton families. When he told Addie about it, she gazed at him skeptically. Unperturbed, Ben shrugged and said, "Anything is possible. We all have to come from *somewhere*. If they go back far enough, who knows?"

Yes, Ben had big plans for Julie. Even bigger than he had let on to Addie. If Grace Kelly, the granddaughter of a Philadelphia bricklayer, could become Princess Grace of Monaco, surely a banker's daughter could aspire to a similar lot.

Only one thing about Julie living with Ben's in-laws mildly compensated for his not having her with him. At least, he reasoned, with Tom and Alice Horton keeping their eagle eyes on her, she couldn't get into any real trouble.

"Now don't build up your expectations too high, dear," Addie cautioned him. "Julie will be just one more young American girl entering the European social set, going to cotillions, to parties, and to country weekends. Just one of many."

"Don't underestimate my position and social contacts," he replied, irritated. "I tell you that *anything* is possible for her. The sky's the limit! Just as long as she's still a virgin. Thank heaven there's no question about that."

One of the doctors started calling Salem General Hospital "Hortonville." Nobody could trace it back to any particular doctor, nor would anyone admit to having been the culprit, but for a while it seemed an appropriate joke.

There was Tom Horton, of course, head of the department of internal medicine and probably the best liked and most respected medical man in the entire county. His son Bill, who had once divided his practice between Salem General and the Upstate Medical Center, had now settled permanently into town. The young surgeon whose fingers had once been so deft had left that field of medicine, and it was too early to tell if he would be the same unquestioned success in a supervisory/administrative capacity.

The third and newest Horton was Dr. Laura Spencer, Mickey Horton's wife. She continued using her maiden name professionally, which was probably just as well. She had also come from the university upstate and had opened a private office and joined the hospital staff only a few months earlier. One of the nurses observed to another that it was entirely possible she didn't know that her brother-in-law was also on staff since he'd returned from California when she was on her honeymoon.

The day she returned to work, a startled Laura found herself sitting opposite Bill Horton at that morning's administrative staff meeting. She and Mickey had flown back to town the night before, too late to call anyone. Mickey had suggested that they take a day to settle in, but Laura had given her word to return the next day. And among psychiatric patients and staff, one's word was never broken.

Glancing at Bill from the corner of her eyes, Laura fought the impulse to blurt out, "If you had the least consideration, you might have . . ." Then she realized that if he'd had the slightest consideration, he wouldn't have left so abruptly or stayed away without a word in the first place. Her psychiatric training told her Bill was merely being consistent.

Bill feasted his eyes upon Laura, all the while desperately wanting to say, "If only I had called, or come back sooner, or done anything to keep in touch, none of this might have happened." But he didn't, and it had, so he kept silent.

With masterful self-control, Laura smiled vaguely at Bill's side of the table without looking at him or even acknowledging his presence.

With an inner excitement, Bill told himself that if she really loved Mickey, and he himself meant nothing to her now, Laura would be able to make eye contact with him. But she couldn't.

For a man with light coloring and dark blond hair, Bill knew he had the darkest, most brooding eyes. Many women had remarked about their depth and power. He'd learned long ago how to use his looks to his advantage. They were what had first attracted Laura to him when they were both at Upstate Medical School.

The heavy-lidded, brooding surgeon, upon whose shoulders rested an awesome weight of responsibility. The serious, somber virtuoso of the operating room, in whose hands lives were placed every day. That had been his image, and he'd adored it. If losing it hadn't meant so much, he never would have fled to California.

But he was a different man now. His ego, it was true, was a little shaky without a scalpel in his hand. He would bide his time, but, if he and Laura were meant for each other, nothing as trivial as a wedding band would keep her away from him for long.

He opened a new pack of little cigars, took one out, and lit it. Exhaling a mouthful of smoke, he watched it float high above the conference table. Then he lowered his eyes to gaze intensely, broodingly, in Laura's direction before returning his attention to the speaker.

The meeting was gradually winding down. Charts were being rolled up. Doctors were being paged over the public address system. Laura, who had been more shaken than she cared to admit by Bill's sultry gaze, was the first to exit.

All day Laura thought about the situation but was unable to resolve it. She had never imagined that she and Bill would find themselves working in the same hospital after all that had happened. It was what they'd once hoped for and planned on, but now it was turning into a nightmare.

Although not as large as the Upstate Medical Center, Salem General was a good-sized hospital. But it was still like a small town. Aptly, Laura was reminded of the cowboy movies she'd seen as a child, where one gun fighter would tell another to get out of town since the town wasn't big enough for the two of them. She wondered which would be the one to go in this case.

She'd already cut her ties once to get away from Bill—when she'd left Upstate. She'd felt then that he might return someday and hadn't wanted to be there if he did. But now she no longer had only herself to think about and plan for. Mickey's law practice was centered in Salem.

"Dr. Horton is paging you, Dr. Spencer,"

said a little nurse who'd come silently up behind her. Laura jumped. Gingerly she picked up the phone, surprised to find her father-in-law on the other end.

"I had to make an emergency call and missed the meeting earlier in the day," he said. "So I thought I'd call now to welcome you back. How was the honeymoon?"

Laura was so relieved that it was the *senior* Dr. Horton that she chattered away like a magpie, telling him all about the honeymoon and how happy they were.

Later that evening, when she and Mickey discussed the day's events, he brought up his brother. "I understand that the wanderer has returned to the fold. Dad called to welcome me back and told me all about it."

Laura hesitated before replying. She'd known the subject would come up but had no idea how she'd handle it. "So many things happened today that I . . . I almost forgot about it," she finally said. "I've told you how busy it was. First day back on the ward and I had to deal with an attempted suicide, mysteriously missing medication, and an undertrained, hysterical psychiatric nurse someone hired in my absence."

"My poor baby," Mickey said, nuzzling her cheek and placing his arms around her. Laura sighed contentedly and nestled her head on his shoulder. Mickey kissed her tenderly on the temple, then hugged her fiercely. How he loved her! And how important it had become to him that she have his child. His mind had often wandered at work as he dreamed of becoming a father. He pictured Horton & Horton stenciled in gold on his office door. Boy or girl, it didn't matter since more and more women were considering law these days.

Hours later, when the lights were out for the night and the alarm was set for the morning, Bill's name came up again.

"Darling . . ." Mickey said in a half whisper.

"Yes, dear?" Laura answered sleepily.

"You never did tell me about your meeting with Bill. Was it friendly? I hope it wasn't strained."

"Actually, it was neither. It was the usual administrative meeting, with tons of people seated at a huge conference table. He wasn't even within speaking distance. We were being lectured to, so there was no time to say hello. And when the meeting ended, my beeper went off." Laura rationalized the last, as her little white lie. She'd willed her beeper to go off, and when it hadn't, she'd gotten up and left anyway, just as though it had.

"Oh," Mickey said, sounding relieved. "And that's when all those crazy people started acting up."

"Yes, dear. But I wish you wouldn't say 'crazy people.' It's not very nice—and it's not even the right term. Someone could sue you for slander," she teased. Then, her mind on Bill again, Laura added, "I don't see myself running into your family very much at the hospital. The psychiatric ward is in a separate wing, you know."

Then, just about to fall asleep, she heard Mickey give a sigh of relief.

Laura soon found out what a small town Salem General Hospital actually was. Whenever she stopped into the cafeteria for coffee or a snack, Bill was there. When she requested the screening room to run a filmstrip on the latest psychiatric innovations, Bill was nearby, checking inventory on films concerning surgical techniques. Laura tried to restrict herself to the psychiatric wing and even took to eating at her desk. She began to feel as confined as her patients. Nevertheless, there were corridors to be traversed, lobbies to be crossed, general meetings to be attended. And everywhere she went, she ran into Bill Horton.

At first it had seemed casual. Then, accidental. Now she'd decided it was part of a well-planned campaign on Bill's part to bait her. He was obviously obsessed with getting a rise out of her for some reason, and any strong reaction on her part would merely feed his obsession. How he accomplished this was beyond her. She only knew that if she thought about it enough, *she* would be the one with the problem.

Laura pored over her medical texts on obsessive-compulsive neuroses, but nothing she read helped to relieve her mind. It was possible, she conceded, that Bill was unable to shake off insistent, repetitive, irrational thoughts about her. As long as they remained unstated thoughts, she might be able to ride it out. But the case histories cited in the texts rarely stopped there.

Laura realized she'd need to face and cope with the situation. Certainly there was no one she could confide in. Besides, there was nothing she could actually point to in the way of antisocial behavior—just a general, overpowering foreboding that followed her from one day to the next . . . like the footsteps that dogged hers through the long, cavernous marble corridors of Salem General Hospital.

"I guess it's not often that you get so personal with someone right out of the blue," Mark said shyly. He was seated with Marie on the back patio of the little cottage she had shared with Tony so rapturously just a few months earlier. At the time, the salesman had told them they were getting a break on the price because it was really too small for more than two people. "But this way," he'd added with a broad smile, "as soon as you decide to have kids, I hope you'll return to my real estate office for a good buy on a roomier place."

No, Marie thought to herself, remembering the conversation, we never had the time to think of raising a family. Then she shook herself out of her reverie to concentrate on Mark. In a way, without his memory *he* was like a child —a lost child, with neither family nor roots. Putting Mark back in touch with himself would be an exciting challenge.

Misinterpreting her silence for disapproval, Mark continued, trying to dispel any awarkwardness. "Maybe we shouldn't get personal after all. I'm sorry if I . . ."

Marie waved aside his words with a friendly gesture. "That's what it's all about, Mark, getting down to basics, helping you to discover everything you once knew. You're like a baby from another planet in one of those science fiction movies."

"Well," he smiled. "Don't plan on adopting me or treating me like a child. I'm years older than you, you know."

Marie wished he hadn't mentioned that. Now that they'd been working together for several sessions, she was beginning to grow fond of Mark. It would be better for all concerned if they kept their relationship on a schoolmarm-schoolboy level.

The session that day included a geography lesson. Mark recited a list of all the states, trying to see if any of them held a special meaning for him. "California," he said at last. "But that's because I spent so many months there at the VA Hospital and then with the Red Cross. And—wait a minute," he added. "San Francisco, too, I guess, because it was the launching pad for every soldier going to Korea."

He couldn't remember what books he'd read as a child until he and Marie visited the local library. Thoughtfully he examined one title after the other, generally recognizing books that she herself had once enjoyed. When Mark observed that they even had the same taste in books, Marie blushed and turned shyly away from him.

Leaving the library, they spontaneously and unconsciously held each other's hand. As soon as she realized it, Marie pulled away and Mark walked silently for a few minutes, his head down, his eyes staring at the sidewalk. "I don't blame you," he finally said. "I've got nothing to call my own—no face, no name, not a damn thing. For all we know, I could be a thief, a killer, a liar—any or all of 'em." He kicked a large stone out of his way impatiently and lengthened his stride to widen the distance between them.

Devastated by the impression she had inadvertently created, Marie ran after Mark and grabbed him by the arm, protesting and apologizing and blushing until he could not doubt her sincerity.

"Okay, okay, Marie, I believe you," he said, then added as an afterthought, "I couldn't have been a very big criminal or the FBI would have caught me by now. Can you picture it? Faces of the nine most wanted men in America on the post office wall. The tenth? Well, if it were me, it would have to be one big bandage with slits for the eyes, tip of the nose, and mouth."

By now Marie could tell when Mark was joking, even without his features to guide her. His soft, raspy voice slid into a pretty good imitation of James Cagney as he ordered a make-believe bank teller to "reach for the sky." Then another voice, this time sounding like Humphrey Bogart, told the Cagney character that the bank was

surrounded and ordered him to "throw out
the gun and come out with your hands up."

Both of them began laughing. "Wherever
it was you grew up," Marie said, still
laughing, "you probably spent most of your
time at the movies. Unless you were a
professional comedian."

Mark shook his head no. He couldn't say
anything for a few moments. He'd been
laughing very hard, and that had set off a
coughing fit. His vocal cords had been
damaged in prison and his "normal" voice
was now a raspy whisper. But, he pointed
out, it enhanced his imitation of James
Cagney. "Although I guess my Bogart just
won't make it."

Marie giggled. "Well, we love you just the
way you are," she reassured him.

By this time they had returned from the
library and were seated on the patio. Mark
reached for her hands, held them gently in
his, and said, "Do you, really, Marie?"

She blustered a bit, then admitted that
she'd been speaking for all of them—her
brother Bill, the people helping him at the
hospital, the surgeons, everyone. Mark
continued to hold her hands, and she didn't
try to break free. She thought to herself that
she would feel silly doing so, but the truth
was she liked the feeling of her hands in his.

"Well," Mark said softly, "I'm proud to say
I love you. I'm not talking about the *plural*
you, the *hospital* you, the *aggregate* you. I
mean the personal, particular, and
wonderful Marie." Marie bit her lip in an

effort not to reply, and after a moment, Mark continued in a lighter tone, "But I won't push my luck by saying any more. I'm ready to get on with the geography lesson as soon as you are."

Chapter Four

A Violation of Trust

Laura Spencer was the prettiest woman Tom Horton had seen in his office in ages. As she leaned back in the chair beside his desk and stretched her long, shapely legs, Tom was able to fully appreciate the attractiveness of this woman who had captured the hearts of two of his sons. In *his* day, or so it had seemed to him, women had been shorter and stockier and nowhere nearly as attractive. And, he'd already fallen in love with Alice by the time he'd begun medical school so he had hardly noticed any other woman because he was so wrapped up in her.

"I still say it's too early to concern yourself with this sort of test," Tom said, smiling at Laura.

"You have my vote on that," Laura replied. "But Mickey is getting so impatient that I agreed to a sterility test just to put his mind at ease. We're both perfectly healthy, so I don't anticipate any problems. She tapped the side of the desk and added, "Knock wood."

Tom laughed in a kindly manner at this hint of superstition from a sophisticated, scientifically trained psychiatrist. Laura merely shrugged and smiled.

The simple test was performed a few minutes later, and after chatting a while longer, Tom suggested that Laura check back "in a week or two or three."

"There's no rush, really," Laura remarked. "Has Mickey made an appointment yet?"

Tom consulted his appointment calendar. "A week from today," he replied. "Our schedules conflict until then." He looked once more at Laura, this time noticing the dark circles under her eyes. The lines of tension around her mouth hinted at a weariness and anxiety that shouldn't have been in a successful young woman recently back from her honeymoon. Tom was certain that Mickey and Laura truly loved each other. He was also pretty sure, as Laura herself appeared to be, that she had nothing to worry about—at least with respect to the sterility test.

Perhaps it's a problem at work, Tom guessed, frowning slightly. But from all accounts, her private practice is thriving and he hadn't heard anything bad about her at the hospital.

All these thoughts passed through Tom's mind just before Laura left his office. During this same time Laura was examining Tom's kindly, open face. She recalled hearing the hospital staff rave about him—particularly his understanding and compassion. Her problem with Bill had intensified in the past few days, to the point where she would have welcomed some advice. But almost as quickly as the thought cropped up, she dismissed it. Tom's desktop and bookshelves were filled with pictures of all his children, each one a treasure. You don't tell a father that one of his treasures may have pathological tendencies.

A look of weariness flickered across her face, then was replaced immediately by a warm smile and a few parting words of thanks. Tom immediately sensed that Laura was not open to any questions or solicitude— at least not right then. After all, she was still a pretty new member of the Horton family. He'd simply have to be patient and welcome any confidences when they were offered. Meanwhile, without actually prying, he'd see how things were progressing at the hospital.

Laura marched briskly out of Tom's office, picked up her briefcase from the receptionist, and headed for her car. Once she had driven away, her shoulders slumped defensively in anticipation of returning to the hospital—to Bill. Without saying a single objectionable word, he had finally succeeded in wearing her down. Had this been a day devoted solely to her private practice, Laura would have been her usual upbeat self. But she was dreading a meeting she had to go to—another strategy of Bill's. He was still showing his obsessive-compulsive persistence—dogging her footsteps or anticipating her direction then preceding her there. His latest ploy had been to actually request her attendance at a meeting of the surgical team. Several other doctors had also been asked, and by casually poking around, Laura had been able to confirm that they planned to attend. So, reluctantly, she'd penciled the meeting in on her calendar.

The meeting was already in progress when Laura slipped into the back of the conference room. She was relieved when several of her colleagues looked around and smiled at her. She saw Bill glance at her out of the corner of his eye, but she was sure no one else had caught the slight movement. He didn't even break his stride as he walked around the screen with a long pointer to isolate specific areas of interest on the illuminated slides.

Every eye in the room was on Dr. William Horton, once a brilliant young surgeon and now temporary administrative head of surgery at Salem General Hospital. Taking full advantage of the spectacular lighting afforded him by the illuminated slides, he loped easily back and forth, indicating a ridge here, a fissure there, a bone that needed replacing.

"For you latecomers," he announced, "we have been examining slides of the face, neck, and chest area of a most challenging patient. I thought I'd review what had already been done for this patient before he arrived in Salem, and then go over what we expect to do, in slow stages, during the next several months."

Interns and residents leaned forward, to better absorb their idol's words of wisdom. To them, Dr. William Horton was a legend. They'd heard tales of the miracles he'd performed when he was a surgeon—a surgeon who was truly king of the hill. Laura had once asked him if he ever got nervous realizing that one wrong cut along a facial nerve could permanently paralyze a patient's entire face. But the scalpel had become an extension of his hand, and he didn't fear it. The scalpel had never let him down—but his hand had.

The patient Bill was lecturing on was Mark Brooks. The slides he was using were of the procedures that had been performed on the West Coast to remove the burned and dead skin. Then, by highlighting a series of thin lines, he indicated what would have to be cut and what could be left on a face more than decimated by burning, battering, and torturing.

Laura marveled at the aloof, impersonal manner Bill projected to the world. In their intimate moments together, she had once found him to be sensuous, possessive, and all-consuming.

Finally the last picture faded from the screen and the lights went up. Bill thanked everyone for coming, then asked one of the surgeons and Laura to remain behind for a minute. He handed the surgeon a file folder and asked them both to walk with him back to his office.

Laura protested, "I really don't see what I—"

"Don't underestimate your importance, Dr. Spencer," Bill interrupted with a smile, gallantly holding open the conference room door for her.

After a slight hesitation, Laura shrugged and preceded the two men into the corridor. When they reached his office, Bill located a second folder, which he handed to the surgeon for examination. Then he turned to Laura and continued conversationally, "As I'm sure you know, an anesthesiologist has to visit a patient the night before an operation to get all the information possible on that patient's general health. Well, I'd like to implement a related procedure—a psychiatric evaluation—to help me gain a more thorough understanding of the patient's mental and emotional health." He stopped talking long enough to wave good-bye to the other surgeon, who had finished examining the pictures and was leaving.

Laura felt unaccountably nervous. This was the first time the two of them had been face to face alone in a room since she'd been married. Bill continued to chat pleasantly about his new procedure as he closed and locked the door, and pulled down the shade on the glass top half of the door. Surely he's not going to dim the lights and show more slides, Laura thought.

She didn't have to wonder long. Suddenly

a firm, strong hand was clamped over her mouth and part of her nose, barely giving her room enough to breathe. She was pushed down on Bill's long, tufted-leather sofa. Then, with an elbow pressing into her ribs to pin her down, Bill tore off her clothing.

For the first time in her life, Laura experienced what several of her patients had told her about—she was brutally and matter-of-factly raped.

When it was over, as Laura sat shaking, pulling her blouse around her shoulders, and trying to locate her shoes and stockings, she watched Bill Horton through eyes swollen with tears. Meticulously he buttoned up his shirt and straightened his tie in the mirror. Then he ran a comb through his hair. Finally he turned to her and said, "Stay as long as you like, *Mrs.* Horton." He shook his head sorrowfully. "What a shame you allowed my poor brother to persuade you to share his name. It's second best, you know . . . If you'd waited, you could have had *me*."

Laura could not stop shivering. And she dared not speak. The man facing her might be her ex-fiancé, but he was also a madman. Anything she said could easily set him off again.

As he picked up his briefcase, he remarked, "I didn't take all I was entitled to. You and Mickey were a little too quick for me. But I won't be bothering you again. And that, my dear, is a promise."

Laura closed her eyes and braced herself for the slamming of the door. When she opened them again, the door was closed and she was alone. She rushed to pick up the phone, hesitated, then put it down again. Whom could she call? What would she say?

Returning to the sofa, she dressed herself as neatly as she could. She turned on the cold water in the sink and let it run over her wrists, then ran a comb through her hair. She tried to apply lipstick, but her hands were shaking so hard she finally gave it up. Then she grabbed an old raincoat of Bill's off the rack, threw it over her shoulders, and ducked out to the parking lot.

When she arrived home, she drew a hot bath and sat soaking for as long as she could, running more hot water every few minutes. Then she called her secretary and told her to cancel her appointments for the rest of the day. "I think I'm coming down with something," she said, her voice sounding genuinely hoarse. "I have a fever and can't keep anything down."

When Mickey came home that evening, she was asleep. She'd left a note on her bedside table next to the phone, saying the same things she'd told her secretary, and adding, "So I really think you ought to sleep in the spare room, darling, if only for tonight. I'd hate to have you catch whatever it is, too."

The next morning, Mickey left before Laura awakened. He had an early appointment and a long day ahead of him. He resolved to call later to check on her and left a love note to cheer her up.

An hour after he'd gone, Laura rose and showered. She stood for a long time under the stinging spray, reveling in the feel of the hot water as it pounded her shoulders and cascaded down her back. Then she dressed and gathered together the borrowed raincoat and every item of clothing she'd worn the day before, throwing it all into an old pillowcase. Reaching under her bed, she located the smart new snakeskin shoes she'd worn for the first time yesterday and put them in too. On her way to the office, she dropped the entire bundle off at the town dump, tossing it into a pile of burning refuse.

Over the next several days, Laura received a number of messages from Dr. William Horton. All her secretary could tell her was that he'd called and would like to speak with her. Laura's secretary had been with her for a substantial period of time and, in Laura's opinion, was completely trustworthy. So after the fifth message, Laura called the woman in to give her further instructions. "From now on, I do not intend to speak with Dr. William Horton or communicate with him in any way."

"Do you want me to tell him that when he calls?"

"No. Quite the contrary. When he calls, be absolutely impersonal. Take his messages as if he were one of those infernal drug salesmen you're so fond of." The secretary grinned and nodded. "Okay. That's about it I guess," Laura said. "I don't think I have to spell it out for you any more than that."

The secretary shook her head and turned to leave. "Oh—one thing more." Laura phrased her words carefully. "Since we've worked together these past few years, you've come to know Bill pretty well, both as a brilliant young surgery resident upstate and, for a brief time, as my fiancé."

The secretary sat down again. thinking this might become serious.

"I am now talking woman to woman," Laura continued, "and I want this to go no further. Bill has been exhibiting . . . well, let's call it troubled signs of an emotional nature since he returned from California. If I thought that they would interfere with his professional judgment, I would do something about it immediately. But I don't. However, I do think he may be having problems . . . relating to women, both inside and outside the workplace. Until I'm satisfied that he has resolved these problems, I would advise you not to be alone with him at any time. Have I gotten through to you?"

"Yes, Dr. Spencer. I read you loud and clear. And, Doctor . . ." The secretary hesitated, not wanting to overstep her bounds. Finally, however, her respect and affection for her boss overrode all other concerns, and she added, "If Doctor Bill ever so much as lays a finger on you, I'm gonna make him wish he hadn't."

Laura smiled ruefully to herself as her secretary left the room. It was a little too late for that, but she appreciated the woman's loyalty and concern.

She had given the incident a great deal of thought once she'd recovered from the initial trauma. By speaking to her secretary, she had only partially resolved her dilemma. She might be able to avoid being alone with Bill from now on, but other women would come in contact with him too. Of one thing she was absolutely sure—she would have to have some sign from Bill that his treatment of her had been a temporary, unique aberration, triggered by a combination of events that would *never* recur.

Laura had therefore decided to wait before saying anything more to anybody. Salem General was inextricably involved with the Hortons—the entire family could be affected if she were to expose one of them in such a manner. Their faces rose up before Laura's troubled mind—kindly Tom; lively, nervous Alice; sensitive Marie; and above all, her loyal, trusting husband. Laura asked herself if she could bear the responsibility of pitting one brother against the next. Such a situation would be unthinkable.

It wasn't long before Bill Horton realized what was happening to his messages. Laura's secretary greeted him on the phone with all the warmth of a robot. None of his calls was returned. The letters he sent were returned unopened. The notes he placed in her mailbox at the hospital somehow found their way back to his mailbox. With each rejection his self-loathing intensified.

When Bill had left Laura cowering and naked on his tufted-leather couch, he'd rushed out of the hospital, gotten into his car, and driven to the first of a series of seedy bars on the other side of town. He had no memory of getting home, but when he awakened the next day, more hung over than he'd ever been in his life, the memory of his hideous deed obliterated all else from his mind.

Finally he'd regained control of himself and downed several cups of coffee. He'd called in sick and stayed home, trying to decide how he could make up for what he'd done. His first instinct had been to run away. Then he'd reminded himself that he'd lost Laura that way. Besides, he had a responsibility now—Mark Brooks. He could not desert the young man after having transported him thousands of miles from the VA Hospital, the Red Cross, and the only life he could remember. When his secretary buzzed to remind him that Mark would be coming in that afternoon, Bill decided not to reschedule. He would continue his work at the hospital as if nothing had happened and try to make amends to Laura any way he could.

If Laura made an official complaint, he would admit to the rape and accept whatever punishment the law required—even if it meant losing his medical license and spending several years in jail. No sentence would be too harsh . . . nothing could ever erase the foul deed from his mind. He still had no idea what had possessed him, but he knew he would never do it again.

During the next several days he concentrated on supervising the various departments under his jurisdiction as well as preparing Mark Brooks for additional surgery. His colleagues and assistants marveled at his stamina and dedication. Especially since any request for help or advice was promptly met.

But all the while, the unanswered messages and returned letters of apology piled up—until finally he could stand it no longer. He picked up the phone, dialed the pathology department, and spoke to his father's closest friend, the head of the pathology lab, Dr. Conrad.

"Are you afraid?" Marie asked Mark as they sat in her patio.

He puffed out his chest and replied in a slight midwestern twang, "Afraid? Me? Don't know the meaning of the word!"

Marie wasn't sure whom Mark was imitating or what movie the line came from, but she sensed that underneath the bravado, he had some qualms about the upcoming operation.

Mark caught the look of concern on her face and said in his own voice, "After what I went through in that prison camp, this should be easy." Then he added jokingly, "Unless they send in a North Korean to operate on me." He imitated a soldier holding up a machete, ready to strike.

Marie giggled. Mark had a marvelous way

of making her laugh, taking her mind off her own problems. At first she'd felt sorry for him. Now she just felt that he was cute and funny and . . . lovable. It took a special kind of courage to emerge from the tortures of hell with a sense of humor.

"I'm crazy about that laugh of yours, my merry Marie," Mark said as they began their walk.

Marie whirled around and stared at him. "Why did you call me that?" she demanded.

"Because you're cute and pretty and merry—and I'm crazy about you," he replied lightly.

"Seriously . . ."

"You mean my being seriously crazy about you?" he teased.

"Please stop that, Mark." Because his emotions so reflected the feelings she herself could not yet face, she generally tried to dismiss Mark's affection whenever he voiced it. This time, however, something else was at issue. "Why not 'cute Marie,' or 'pretty Marie,' if it's all the same to you? Nobody has called me 'merry Marie' since I was a little girl in grade school."

They walked silently for a block or two. Then Mark said, "I won't say it again if it bothers you. You just looked very merry to me, and the name seemed to fit. Maybe it's part of the lyric of an old pop song I once knew years ago, in another life."

They were headed for the local library to return some books when suddenly Marie veered left. Mark followed her, slightly disoriented. She'd decided earlier that the library's main branch might have more of a literary selection, but she'd been too preoccupied to mention it. Now, still disturbed by Mark's innocent remark, she was unaware of Mark's growing puzzlement. "Did Bill arrange for you to see Laura?" she asked abruptly, changing the subject.

"Nope. At first he wanted her to decide if I was strong enough emotionally to deal with all the cutting and slicing. Then I guess he decided I was, all by himself."

"Laura's a very smart woman," Marie commented.

"So are you. You don't give yourself half the credit you deserve."

"That's what my family always says. You're beginning to sound more like them every day."

"Are we going to the main branch of the library?" Mark asked.

"Yes . . . how did you know?"

"You said we were off to the library, and this is not the direction we took the other day."

It made sense, except that an odd feeling flashed through Marie. They stopped at the main branch only long enough to return several books. Marie had forgotten that it was Thursday, the day she usually dropped by her father's office to update his files. She'd told him she wouldn't have much time this week, but on a hunch, she decided to go there now anyway.

Mark was perfectly agreeable. As long as

he was with Marie, anything was fun. Together, he felt, the two of them had built up a life that was becoming precious to him, of little walks and errands and meanderings. Alone, anything he did was uneventful. With Marie, everything was fun, meaningful, worthwhile.

Marie felt it too — even though she couldn't quite admit it to herself . . . yet. But she'd taken to dreaming about Mark, and that made her feel very guilty. Over and over she asked herself how she could possibly let anyone replace Tony in her thoughts and dreams.

As they rounded the corner leading to the big colonial structure that was both the Horton house and Tom's private office, Mark stopped swinging Marie's hand. It was high noon and both family cars were out, which meant no one was at home, Marie turned the lock on the office door, and the two of them entered.

"I won't be long," Marie promised. Quickly she sorted through a pile of unopened letters, marking some, discarding others. Mark looked around, thumbed through some magazines, and then followed Marie into the inner office. As she neatly arranged the letters and magazines on her father's desk, Mark examined the various family photographs positioned around the room. "That's Bill all right," he commented. "He doesn't look as if he's changed too much."

"That's Addie," Marie said. "She's Julie's

mother. You remember meeting my niece, Julie."

"Mickey?" Mark asked, picking up another framed picture.

Marie nodded, wondering when Mark had met her brother Mickey. Next Mark picked up a slightly blurred shot of Tommy Horton, whom Marie could barely remember. He had been sent to Korea when she was still a child. Looking at his picture in Mark's hand gave her an inexplicable feeling of sadness . . . and foreboding.

"Another brother?" he asked.

Marie nodded. Another brother, same war. The possibility crossed her mind that the two could have known each other.

Suddenly Mark groped for the edge of the desk to steady himself, still clutching the picture. Then he eased himself down into the comfortable sofa. Marie heard him make a strange sound that puzzled her for a minute. It started as a rumble, grew to a spasm . . . and then she knew Mark was sobbing.

"What is it, Mark?" she asked gently. "All those memories of Korea?" She wanted to put her arms around him to comfort him, but he waved her away.

Marie finished what she was doing, then waited patiently until Mark pulled himself together. Without a word they put all the pictures back in place and left, locking the door behind them.

Mark walked very slowly on the way back to the cottage, and Marie matched her pace with his. He didn't reach for her hand or say a word. For a while, neither did she.

"Are you thinking of the upcoming surgery? Are you concerned?" Marie asked quietly.

He shook his head. "Just as long as they knock me out before they wheel me into the operating room, I'll be fine."

They walked a few more blocks in silence. When they reached the gate to Marie's patio, Mark said, "I don't think I'll be needing to work with you anymore, Marie. This is probably our last session."

The sadness in his voice overwhelmed her. "What's wrong, Mark?"

"Nothing's wrong. You did what you set out to do. You gave me back my memory."

Marie looked at him in bewilderment. "You mean back at my father's? When you saw the pictures?"

He nodded. "Marie, that was *me* that I was looking at! . . . Don't you understand? I'm Tommy Horton. Bill is my brother—and you . . . you're my sister."

Chapter Five

The Best Laid Plans...

Mickey and Laura toasted each other with champagne. "You are the best thing that ever happened to me," Mickey said, kissing her for the dozenth time that hour. "And the cleverest thing, too," he added.

"You deserve some of the credit, you know," Laura countered playfully. "You don't have to have an M.D. to know that it takes two to make a baby."

Laura had called Mickey as soon as her obstetrician had confirmed the pregnancy. Since he'd been in a meeting at Woodridge Industries, his secretary had obligingly transferred the call. Then, because of a telecommunications mix-up, Laura's voice had come in loud and clear over the conference line so that all of the men in the room as well as Mickey had heard the exciting news. The conference had broken up with laughter and boisterous congratulations, and each man had given Mickey a special toast. Then they'd slapped him on the back and sent him home to his wife, telling him that all other business could wait.

"Weren't you embarrassed?" Laura asked, laughing.

"With anyone else I might have been. But those guys were so loyal to me during that lawsuit that they're almost like my own family." He kissed her again, then sighed contentedly. This was a day he had dreamed of for years, longed for every time he'd visited anyone with small children. Now he felt that all his prayers had been answered.

"See?" Laura pointed out. "You don't need to get a sterility test after all. Now we have proof positive!"

"It's just been that my mind's been so preoccupied with work that I've forgotten to tell you. I'm sorry, darling. Actually, I did get one the other day. I'd had to postpone it once, then Dad had to go out of town unexpectedly, but we finally worked it out." He poured more champagne. "That reminds me, should we call home and tell them the good news?"

"It's customary to wait a while so that the parents-to-be have a chance to get used to the idea. But since it's already been broadcast over a conference line . . ."

They both laughed and decided to wait a day or two before sharing the news with the family. It wouldn't be Mickey's parents' first grandchild, but it would be *their* first child, and they felt as proud as if they'd invented the world.

They waited till the weekend to call Alice. Mickey got on one extension and Laura on the other, so that they could share Alice's delighted reaction. They made her promise not to tell anyone the news for a while. "You'll at least let me tell Dad, won't you?" Alice asked eagerly. Mickey and Laura laughed and told her of course she could.

When Alice excitedly broke the good news to Tom, she thought at first he looked a little subdued, even puzzled. Then he told her how pleased he was, and she decided he was simply tired and overburdened. "You have to take more time off from your work," Alice told him firmly. "You're not a young man anymore, you know."

Tom had been planning to make one last trip to his office that weekend to check a couple of papers in his files. But after Alice's remark, he decided that, rather than start an argument, it might be wiser to wait until Monday. But he was sure it would prove to be one of the longest weekends in his memory. And unless he'd completely lost that memory, the information in those papers would make it necessary to set up another appointment with Laura—one he wouldn't be looking forward to.

"It reminds me of those glorious days I spent in the south of France," the duchess commented to Addie. "When I was a girl we loved to vacation there and eat bowl after bowl of bouillabaisse. Of course, *this* is just fish soup. In order to be called bouillabaisse, it has to be made with those special fish that seem to swim only in Marseilles." She stuffed a huge spoonful in her mouth and after swallowing it mumbled, "I really can't tell the difference. This is easily as good." Then she smacked her lips and made a little sound, which among the less royal might have been called a hiccup.

The duke patted her indulgently on the back as she continued chattering away. Addie Olson looked amused, but Ben kept a straight face, waiting for an opportunity to get a word in.

"Bouillabaisse, eh?" Ben pounced when the duchess tried vainly to stifle another hiccup. "Know what, Addie? I'll bet Julie would love this soup. Do you think we'll have to fly to the south of France to get her some . . . or perhaps the duchess might ask the cook for the recipe."

I'll—hic!—do better than that," the duchess replied, only slightly incoherently. "While your daughter is—hic!—visiting you in Paris, we'll make a date for you to fly her up here and I'll—hic!—have the cook make it. James will be down from Oxford, and the two might—hic!—meet."

Addie smiled to herself. Ben had been talking about Julie's "imminent" arrival for months now. He mentioned her name everywhere they went, almost as if he were her public relations representative. Even here, at a huge lawn party outside London, where bankers mixed discreetly with royalty to encourage creditors and keep their eye on debtors, Ben couldn't resist bringing up his beautiful, talented, accomplished daughter, who would "love" fish soup. Fish soup indeed! Addie thought to herself with a snort—Julie was a finicky eater and detested fish in any form.

But if it hadn't been that, it would have been something else. He'd told the Dutch banking commissioner how much Julie loved ice skating. "Then we must persuade her to stay until next winter," the banker had replied politely. Unfortunately it turned out that the Dutch commissioner, a confirmed bachelor, was himself bored by women and saw absolutely no reason to foist them on other, less intelligent men. Undeterred, however, Ben dropped Julie's name in other circles within the international banking community.

"Why don't we wait until we actually know that she's coming?" Addie asked. "If you're going to beat the drum for your daughter all over Europe, you might at least wait until we get her flight number."

Ben hated to be reminded of the fact that his Christmas and Easter plans for his daughter had gone awry. Julie had written each time to say that she'd be too busy with schoolwork. But now there could be no more such excuses because summer was coming.

Shortly after they'd been to the lawn party, the Olsons received word that Julie was really coming. They instructed their stateside travel agent to prepare a generous amount of traveler's checks for her and arrange a first-class ticket. Then a call from the travel agent confirmed Julie's flight and arrival time. Soon after these arrangements had been made, they received a letter in Julie's careless scrawl, giving them much the same information. Ben could not control his excitement.

Addie could not control her curiosity.

Ben spent the week preceding Julie's arrival occupying his secretarial and junior banking staff with tasks that were somewhat unusual. Jacques, whose father was a count, compiled a list of all the Parisian soirées and balls taking place within the next thirty days. Hans covered Switzerland and Austria. Ben's private secretary handled the London scene for him as a matter of course, but this time he also had a list of embassies for her to contact and asked her to talk with the bank's public relations staff about putting a word or two in a society column about Julie's arrival.

Addie suggested that Ben might be overdoing it and that they visit quietly with Julie for a few days before sharing her with the international set.

It was a pale, shy, uncertain young woman who greeted her parents in the arrival terminal at Orly. To Addie's practiced eye, Julie looked different, changed somehow. But still *provincial*. The floppy sailor blouse she was wearing might be chic in Salem, but it wouldn't do in Paris. Nevertheless, it made Julie look fragile and feminine, and to Ben, of course, that was all to the best.

Both parents thought it was fortunate that

she had brought virtually nothing. She would be taken immediately to several of the better couturiers and completely outfitted before being introduced to a soul.

Julie kissed each parent gently without giving them her customary bear hug.

Ben assumed that she was tired out from her trip.

Addie thought it was the shock of finding herself on a strange continent for the first time.

Ben had the driver stop the limousine several times on the way back to their Paris flat so that he could point out famous sites. And all the while Julie looked very vague and tense.

When Julie had been shown to her room and the maid had drawn her bath, Addie sat in the living room and smoked while Ben paced.

"She doesn't look well, Addie. Do you think she looks well? Do you think there's anything wrong? What could it be?"

"Why don't you ask her?" Addie replied with studied indifference.

"Because *you're* her mother," he snapped, "that's why! Although if anyone asked me, I'd say that you're not acting like it."

As nobody *was* asking him, Addie kept silent. If anything was on Julie's mind, they'd find out about it soon enough. Julie had a great deal to learn about hiding things, evading questions, or using what men called diplomacy and women knew was common sense.

Before long, Julie was seated in a Louis Quatorze antique satin chair, in a terry cloth robe, with her feet tucked under her and her wet hair pulled back in a ribbon.

Here it comes, thought Addie.

"I'm pregnant," Julie abruptly announced.

Addie felt a chill go through her. She instantly recalled the oversized sailor blouse Julie had arrived in.

Ben exploded, his generally ruddy complexion deepening to a blotchy purple. For a moment Addie thought he was going to have a heart attack.

"Who is he?" he roared. "Who is the— the—" He fought to get the words out without cursing. "Who is the man who has done this to me?"

Addie had to stop herself from laughing hysterically at such a ludicrously self-centered remark. It was so typical of Ben.

Julie squirmed around until her feet hung down and dangled nervously. She stared at the intricate designs on the Persian rug. "Nobody did anything to you, Daddy."

"You know damn well what I mean. Who got you into this condition? Who is the father?"

"His name is David Martin. He was the only man I ever loved or ever hope to love, and Susan killed him."

Slowly the story came out. Fleetingly Ben regretted canceling their subscription to the Salem local paper. But then he thought sarcastically that he didn't need to read about bad news—he could sit right here in his own living room and have it given to him personally.

Addie instinctively began to reach out to comfort Julie. Out of the corner of her eye she saw Ben shaking his head, signaling her to stay where she was and let him handle things. This was a "big" decision, and according to their agreement, Addie was to leave everything up to him.

Ben eyed his daughter coldly. "Why don't you go into your room. You've had a long trip, and we'll accomplish nothing with you sitting here shivering." Although her hair had almost dried and she was wrapped in a thick robe, Julie was indeed shivering. "Go on," Ben ordered sharply. "Your mother and I have a great deal to discuss."

After she left the room, Ben made a show of locking the door, then turned to Addie with a murderous look on his face. He began their "discussion" in a venomous whisper, but his rage soon got the better of him, and before long he was bellowing at the top of his lungs. It was all Addie's fault, because she was a Horton! Mickey was also to blame, as were Tom, Alice, and right on down the line. "I wouldn't trust a broken finger to the Doctors Horton, a parking ticket to the Horton lawyer, or a pure, untouched virgin to any of that cursed family of yours."

Addie's mouth opened in astonishment. In all the years they'd been married, she had never heard such unjustified accusations—such hateful *slander*—spew forth from Ben Olson's mouth. At first she wanted to pack her own bags as well as her daughter's and fly back to Salem, leaving Ben to stew in his own fury. Then she had second thoughts.

If she left Ben now, he would call it desertion. He had the means to hire the finest lawyers in the world, and they could probably work it so that she didn't get a dime. Addie had spent many years basking in wealth and luxury, and she had no desire to be poor the rest of her life. If it would help Julie, she would consider defying Ben. But perhaps she could help Julie more by staying. Perhaps she could save enough from her allowance, even pawn some of her infrequently worn jewelry, to raise the funds her daughter would soon need.

When Ben finished ranting, he rushed to the bathroom. Lately whenever he got excited, his stomach acted up. But stubborn to the last, he did nothing his doctor suggested and glared at Addie if she so much as hinted that he slow down or take his medication.

So knowing that Ben would be occupied for quite some time, Addie took the opportunity to slip in to see Julie. She was staring at the ornate, gilded ceiling, her eyes brimming with tears.

"It's all right, Mom. I should have expected it. I never should have come here at all."

"What will you do, darling?"

"I don't know."

"Daddy is arranging a flight out of here for tomorrow. I'm going to call Grandma Alice.

She'll meet you at the airport and drive you to Great-Aunt Martha's. Mothers are supposed to be wise. Well, I've made more than *my* share of mistakes. But *my* mother, *your* Grandma Alice, will know just what to do. She helped Great-Aunt Martha's daughter years ago."

Julie looked up, eyes wide with astonishment. "Aunt Sally?" she asked.

"Yes, baby. But don't you ever repeat that to a soul."

From far away, Ben could be heard yelling, "Addie? I need those pills. *Addie?* Where are you?"

Addie leaned down and kissed Julie on her cheek.

"Mom?"

"What, darling? I must run."

"How can you stand him after all he said?"

"He doesn't mean it, dear. He's just upset."

Julie had heard that all her life—it was the one thing that never changed. After her mother had left, she closed her eyes and tried to get some sleep. Another long trip tomorrow, she thought. At this rate, I'm beginning to feel like a stewardess.

Hours later the arguing began again. Julie awakened to hear Ben bellow to Addie that his daughter had destroyed his life. "Whatever happens," he continued furiously, "she's not going to destroy my good name!"

His, his, him, him! Julie thought sleepily. *I'm* the one who's going to have the baby!

She heard the door slam and remembered the thousands of times she'd heard that sound before, and then promptly fell asleep again.

For eleven-year-old Sandy Horton life was just one chore after another. When she did poorly in school, her mother told her that she was lazy and stupid, just like her father. For all Sandy knew it could have been true. Her dad had been drafted and sent to Korea when she was a baby, so she had no way of knowing how bright or energetic he might have been.

Her mother, Kitty, was no great shakes herself is what Sandy often thought after she'd been given a bawling out for something all the other kids did. After all, Sandy reasoned, it's easy to blame Daddy when he's been missing all these years and is probably dead way over there in Korea. It would be different if he were here to defend himself.

This time Sandy decided to take his side. "How dumb could he be when the rest of his family is so smart?" she asked. "One brother is a doctor and the other is a lawyer. That doesn't sound like *dumb* to me!"

This, Sandy knew, was the easiest way to get a rise out of her mother. Just mention her in-laws and Kitty Horton was ready to explode. They had never treated her properly, she felt. Coming from a poor mill town upstate, Kitty was forever self-conscious about her clothes, her conversation, and her lack of "proper" education. When the Hortons had opened their arms to Tommy's new bride, she'd interpreted their warm welcome as "phony." She had never known people to act like that unless they had been after something.

When Tommy was reported missing in action, Tom and Alice Horton invited Kitty and Sandy to stay with them for a while and then offered to help them pick out an apartment nearby if they liked.

Kitty remembered all the holidays she'd spent with them, pressuredly looking around the table to see what fork to use and which glass and salad plate were hers. She had never been able to relax and enjoy a meal with them. She loved a good joke, but she'd stopped telling jokes when she visited the Hortons because no one smiled, or else the smiles were forced. Tommy had later told her that such jokes were fine for the local tavern, but inappropriate for the dinner table. Nobody ever used the term "vulgar," but Kitty was certain that they whispered it behind her back.

No, she didn't like the Hortons, although she was willing enough to take a monthly check from them to subsidize what little the government provided. She told them she'd decided to remain upstate.

Sandy, on the other hand, liked the Hortons. They always remembered her birthday and Christmas with wonderful gifts. Whenever her mother really lost her temper, Sandy would dream of running away to stay with her grandmother. She was sure nobody in Salem would call her dumb or lazy.

Kitty was the lazy one, at least as far as Sandy was concerned. No other child in her class had to do so many errands around the house. Some days Kitty would clutch her chest and moan, "Oh, my heart. Sandy, would you finish the cleaning and cook dinner?"

Sandy didn't exactly believe her mother. Her "attacks" were too conveniently timed—always cropping up when the hardest chores had to be done. It was a great excuse all right, but one that only grown-ups could use. If Sandy tried it, she was sure her mother would drag her to a doctor just to show her up as a liar. Only grown-ups could lie whenever they wanted to, Sandy decided. Especially mothers.

Nobody was happier to hear that Tommy Horton was alive and back in Salem than his daughter, Sandy. As Grandpa had explained, Daddy couldn't come up to see them because he was undergoing tests in the Salem hospital where they were going to fix his face. She and her mother were to pack and come down to Salem, where they would stay at Grandma and Grandpa's. Sandy was going to have Marie's old room all to herself. She couldn't wait!

Chapter Six

Inadmissible Evidence

When Laura received the message to call Dr. Tom Horton, she was in session with a patient and faced with an extremely crowded schedule for the rest of the day. When she finally managed to squeeze in a few minutes to call, she was surprised when he asked her to drop in.

"Gee, Dad, I would have gotten back sooner, but I thought it was just a call to say hello, or maybe to congratulate us. You've heard, haven't you? By now I guess everyone has heard." When Tom said that he had and offered his best wishes, she added playfully, "Mickey is sure that it was having you give us those tests that made all the difference in the world. He calls them your 'good luck' tests. He's so delighted about becoming a father that he can hardly think of anything else."

Tom said all the right things, made all the right answers, but Laura detected a note of strain in his voice. "Is anything wrong?" she asked anxiously. "Do you need to give me another examination or a test of some sort?"

Tom assured her that there was nothing to worry about regarding the pregnancy and, relieved, Laura made an appointment to see him at the end of the day. After she'd hung up, she almost left a message for Mickey to pick her up at his father's, but something told her not to mention the appointment until she'd found out what it was all about. Instead, she simply left word that she would be late.

It was after six when Laura drove up to Tom's private office. The nurse was just leaving as she entered. There were no more patients in the waiting room and the atmosphere had taken on a relaxed, informal quality.

Tom Horton called to her from the inner office. "Come on in, Laura. I was just finishing up. You don't have to close the door. We're all alone here." He stood up as she entered and leaned across his desk to accept a kiss on the cheek. Then he held up two file folders. "These are my last items of business for the day. Once they're out of the way, a weight will have been lifted from my mind."

"And they concern me?" Laura asked, puzzled.

Tom nodded. "The first is your sterility test. As I certainly don't have to tell you after the fact, you've come through with flying colors. You should have a fine, healthy baby if you follow all the usual instructions, and after that, as many more babies as you wish."

Laura waited silently. For the life of her, she couldn't tell what her father-in-law was leading up to.

"Mickey, as you know, came in a couple of weeks after you. The results had just gotten back from the lab when Alice told me about your pregnancy." He handed her Mickey's file. "As you can see from the lab report, Mickey is sterile. He's incapable of biologically achieving fatherhood."

Tom watched as Laura bit her fist to keep from crying out. The look of bewilderment on her face reminded him of some of the teenagers he'd seen at the clinic when he was first practicing medicine—ignorant young girls who'd barely learned the facts of life before discovering they were pregnant. "Babies having babies," Tom had once observed to Alice.

But this was entirely different. Here was a mature, sophisticated, intelligent woman. Surely she knew who had fathered her child.

With a single word, Laura wrenched Tom from his private thoughts. "Bill!" Laura began to sob. "Oh my God, it must have been Bill. When he raped me."

Tom leaned back in his chair and pulled out a bottle of Scotch from the left bottom drawer of the desk. Then, letting Laura sob out all the trauma, all the pain and tension of the past weeks, he filled a bowl of ice from the refrigerator and brought in some paper cups. Laura grabbed the box of tissues sitting on his desk, sniffed, and wiped her eyes. When she spotted the Scotch, she smiled through her tears. "I'll take mine straight, thanks."

Tom poured out a full cup for each of them, then settled back and gestured to Laura to relax and calm herself. He sensed she would unburden herself when she was ready.

Laura looked around at the family portraits and photos Tom had scattered around his desk and on the bookshelves. She picked up a graduation photo of Bill Horton and stared at it for a minute, then turned it face down on the glass top of Tom's desk. She ran her hands through her hair, smoothing it away from her forehead. Finally she leaned forward, chin thrust out resolutely. "None of this must ever get back to Mickey. It would break his heart. Bill has done enough as it is."

Little by little the story began to come out.

"Bill must have been so surprised when he returned and found that I had married," Laura said, then added, "'surprised' would be putting it mildly."

"Let's go back to the beginning," Tom suggested. "Back to when you and Bill were still engaged, upstate." By asking Laura to backtrack a little, Tom hoped to give her a breather, a chance to collect her thoughts and gain control of her emotions before reliving what must have been a harrowing, traumatic experience.

It worked. Laura relaxed as she recalled

how happy they'd been at Upstate Medical Center, planning for their joint future. Then Bill had started getting those mysterious tremors in his right hand. "They were so minuscule, so tiny, that I couldn't even see them. I'll bet you couldn't either," she told Tom. "But Bill went to the head of the neurology department and had him run a series of tests. At one point when the news didn't look good, I told him I loved him and would stay with him and believe in him regardless of the outcome." She paused and looked at Tom. "You know, I don't think that what I said mattered to him in the least. *That* magic hand, *those* five famous fingers, meant more to him than anyone and anything in the world. It was surgery or nothing!"

"The problem never progressed beyond that first stage, did it?" Tom asked quietly.

"No. And the neurologists promised him that it wouldn't. They took electrical measurements of his muscle activity and tried several therapies. In the end, they told him that with the proper rest, the hand would be *almost* as good as new."

Tom recalled the copy he'd received of the medical report. Nodding, he gestured for Laura to continue.

Well, *almost* wasn't good enough for Bill."

"I know that well enough," Tom concurred, sighing. "He was the most competitive child I've ever known. He had to be first and best at everything. And of course, he was. Part of it was intelligence and ability and good looks, everything he was fortunate enough to be born with. But the rest was drive, concentration, and relentless practice."

Laura remembered well how Bill would spend endless hours tying intricate knots in silk thread with just one hand. The right hand.

Tom poured them both another drink. "And when Bill wanted the best," he continued, "his standards were hard to meet. That's why I knew that the girl he chose for his wife would be the brightest and best-looking woman he could find."

"Not bright enough to realize the seriousness of his psychological problems." Laura smiled grimly. "And that, ironically enough, is supposed to be what I'm best at."

"Did you have anything to do with Bill's trip to California?"

She shook her head emphatically. "One day he was there, and the next day he had gone. When his office called me, I referred them downstate to you. The next thing I knew, the California Medical Association contacted the medical center here for his credentials. Then, little by little, more news filtered back, to me—but always through third parties."

Tom leaned over, looking incredulous. "You mean to tell me that son of mine, your fiancé at the time, never contacted you to say where he was, or to ask you to join him?"

"No. I neither heard from him nor saw him until the day I returned from my honeymoon with Mickey. Then, several weeks later, he lured me into his office on a plausible pretext, ripped off my clothes, and raped me."

There! She had said it. And this time she had been composed enough not to burst into tears. Tom led her gently through enough details to get a general picture without prying unnecessarily. Then he asked how she might explain Bill's actions if she were called upon to comment professionally on such a case.

Laura shook her head. "This is too recent, and now affects too many lives. Also, I'm too close to the situation—I'm—too subjective." She paused. "We both know that rape often has more to do with uncontrollable rage and assertions of power than with sex itself. When Bill proposed marriage to me, he was in a sense *claiming* me, the way a gold miner claims a stake. The miner may go off to claim other stakes, might even be gone for years at a time, but that mine he considers his when he returns."

"People aren't gold mines," Tom said.

"That's just part of it," Laura continued. "I was an object to him, awaiting his convenience. I sincerely thought that by leaving so abruptly and never writing or calling, Bill was cutting off his ties with me as well as with the hospital. I was a mess for a long time. Finally I had to leave too, because the place held too many memories. I would still be in a horrible state if I hadn't met Mickey."

Now that Laura had brought Tom up to date, she wondered what he would do. Bill Horton's child was growing within her. The information in the folders could destroy three lives, maybe more, and the only people who knew *all* the facts of the situation were herself—and Tom.

"This would destroy Mickey," Laura said softly. "He's so thrilled with the pregnancy that he's acting like a cartoon character, grinning like a fool and swaggering as if he'd just won the medal of honor. And considering what a decent, likable, dependable guy he is . . . well, no one deserves that magic time more than he does."

Tom realized what a huge quandry it was. He considered the situation for a few minutes, then sighed heavily. "I can't give you an answer now, Laura. If you pressed me at this moment, my instinct would be to bring everything out in the open and let the chips fall where they may. We're doctors— trained scientists. We're supposed to begin with the facts and build a case from there."

Images of a bloody confrontation between the two brothers flashed through Laura's mind. Taking sides in such a fight could cause irreparable damage to the family itself. And what of the child? Laura's eyes filled with tears. Everything she held dear would be destroyed if the baby's paternity were questioned.

As Tom observed Laura's reaction to his remarks, he too found himself burdened with a number of troubling thoughts. Once the story came out, Mickey would insist that Laura bring charges of rape against Bill. Tom was sure of that. And as a result of his brutal assault on Laura, Bill might spend the rest of his life in jail. It would certainly destroy his medical career.

"There's really no rush," he said finally. "What's been done can't be undone, whatever we decide here. We both may feel differently about it all in a few days. Let's leave it as it is for now. I give you my word that news of this will never leave this room . . . at least until we have our next talk."

Alice began setting up the guest room for Kitty Horton, trying to shake the uncomfortable feeling she had every time she contemplated the arrival of her estranged daughter-in-law. She didn't exactly begrudge Kitty hospitality. It was just that Kitty was the sort of person who went about making everyone else feel uncomfortable.

She'd come into the family with a chip on her shoulder, and it had grown harder for the Hortons to dislodge with each passing year. When Tommy had been listed as missing in action, the entire family had comforted her when she was pregnant. They'd inundated her with gifts when the baby arrived and looked for ways to make Kitty's life easier. Nevertheless, the Hortons each separately breathed a sigh of relief when Kitty had rejected their hospitality and returned to her home upstate with her baby daughter.

She would doubtlessly have dragged

Tommy upstate when he "returned," if that were possible. However, all the operations had already been scheduled and were to be performed under Bill Horton's supervision at Salem General Hospital.

When the Horton children were younger and annoyed with Kitty for yelling at them or ordering them about, Marie had once confided to Mickey that perhaps Kitty had an inferiority complex. Mickey, who usually had only kind things to say about people, had retorted that it wasn't a *complex*. She was just inferior and *knew* it—and knew that everyone else knew it too.

Alice had turned away to hide a smile when she'd heard that. With all the nasty things Kitty said about everybody, she'd probably deserved that remark. But Alice wanted all her children to be kind, gracious, and tactful. As Tom had once ruefully pointed out, Kitty could *create* snobbery in others where it had never existed before.

At least the house wouldn't be crowded. By opening up the third floor, Alice was able to provide a bedroom and sitting room for Tommy and Kitty and a separate bedroom down the hall for Sandy. There had been some talk of a family get-together, but for some reason Tom discouraged his family from making any plans. "Let's just take things as they come and try to keep our tempers while they're here," he advised.

"She may have improved during the years Tommy was missing," Alice pointed out hopefully.

Tom shook his head. "I heard part of Tommy's end of the conversation when she called the other day while I was visiting him in the hospital. I really couldn't take it. I walked out of the room to give him some privacy. It sounded as if she wanted him to rip off the bandages, unplug his intravenous tube, and march right back upstate. My heart goes out to that boy."

At first it looked as if Tom had been wrong. The house rang with happiness, despite Kitty's ill will. The difference was Sandy, a youngster who had been given the greatest, most unexpected present in the world—a father. And she wanted to spend every available minute with him.

As for Tommy, he was still coping with the return of his memory. The one person he wanted to talk with about it was Marie. And she was the one person who avoided him.

The entire family had been dumbfounded when Tommy had remembered who he was. They'd heard that Bill was working with a soldier in the hospital but knew little more than that. When Alice found out that he was indeed her own lost son, she hugged him fiercely even though his ribs were bandaged, and exclaimed, "How wonderful that Marie was the one who helped you find your memory. And she was so *young* when you left for the service. She was the baby of the family. It's ironic, and *so* lucky!"

"What are they doing to you, Daddy?" Sandy

asked. Once they'd allowed the young girl to visit her father in the hospital, there'd been no holding her back. Kitty dropped in and out, but Sandy couldn't be pried away.

"Well," Tommy said through his bandages, "remember all those pictures the family has around of me as a kid and me in uniform?" Sandy nodded. "Bill made copies of all of them for the surgeons. That way, when they finish with me and take off all the bandages, you'll recognize me."

"I love you anyway, Daddy."

Tommy answered her in a loving voice, "Since my ribs are bandaged and very sore, consider yourself hugged, kid."

"What did they need your ribs for?" she wanted to know. Tommy started singing, "The rib bone's connected to the jawbone, and the—"

"No, it's not!" Sandy cried, laughing. "The rib is down on your side where the bandage is, and the jawbone is what you're talking with."

Although Tommy continued on in a bantering tone, he was actually telling Sandy the truth. It had sounded simple when Bill had explained it to him. Apparently a large part of his jaw had been shot away, and a certain amount of bone had been removed from his rib to replace it—to actually *restructure* a new jaw. It was just one of a number of incredible procedures that would be done on him to repair all the damage.

When Tommy tried to explain this to Kitty, she held up her hands and made a face.

"Don't tell me! It all sounds so gory. What's going to happen to your rib? Will you be able to work? To lift things?"

"Don't worry, honey," Tommy said. "Bill explained it all to me. I'm still young enough for the rib to heal completely and quite soon. So I'm not losing a rib, I'm just gaining a chin."

Kitty paced up and down the hospital room, annoyed by the explanation. It all sounded too simple, too cut-and-dried, as if someone were trying to put something over on her. "That's all very well and good, if you believe that brother of yours. *I* heard that they kicked him out of Upstate Medical Center and he ran away to California because nobody else would hire him." Kitty stood at the foot of the bed, looking down at her bandaged husband, and sneered. "Is that the sort of man you would trust to engineer this whole thing?"

Tommy tried to lift himself up on his elbows to better confront his wife at eye level. "You're damn right he's the man I would trust—with my face, my ribs, my life." He wanted to say more, but suddenly the energy drained out of him.

"Hi, fella!" Both Tommy and Kitty turned at the sound of Mickey's voice. They realized he must have overheard their conversation, although he made no mention of it. "I can see how bushed you are, so I won't stay." He unwrapped a plant he was carrying and placed it near the window. Then he took a couple of books out of his briefcase and put them on the night table. "Thought they might amuse you. Laura and I picked them out. So long, buddy." As Tommy said good-bye, Mickey turned to Kitty and said, "Can I give you a lift?"

Before she could even think of a reply, Kitty felt Mickey's arm firmly under hers, propelling her out of the room. Looking back, she saw that Tommy's eyes had closed.

When they reached the hospital grounds, Kitty said, "I have my own car, thank you."

"I know you do," Mickey replied. "I merely wanted to take the opportunity to get things straight. I heard what you said to Tommy about Bill. Never slur a professional man, especially one in medicine, law, or the judiciary. A doctor's reputation is sacrosanct. If you ever say anything like that again, I will personally haul you up on charges of slander. You'll be faced with enormous legal bills and a fine that might wipe out your life savings."

Nobody had ever spoken to Kitty like that before. She was speechless. As she began to sputter, Mickey continued calmly.

"For your information, Bill's reputation is tops—both upstate and here. They would take him back in a minute. They've already made several offers. He left only to volunteer his services to his country through the Red Cross. If you stopped spreading ugly rumors long enough to read the papers, you'd find that Bill has become quite the local hero."

Mickey picked up his briefcase, gave her a

mock salute, and climbed into his car, whistling as he drove home. He didn't really know what had prompted him to be so blatant with Kitty. He reasoned that he'd been appalled to overhear her trying to create doubts in a patient's mind about his own doctor. Next, he'd been incensed at the slander she'd so indifferently repeated and had wanted to stop it at its source before it spread any further. And also there was another generation to consider. He smiled. As a father-to-be, he wanted his child to be proud of the Horton family name. This was the only time Mickey could remember having been quite so outspoken. And it hadn't hurt a bit. If anyone had it coming to her, Kitty did.

After Mickey had driven off, Kitty remained seated on a bench for a few minutes, trying to pull herself together. She thought she felt her heart beating irregularly and reached into her pillbox for a nitroglycerine tablet, placing it under her tongue with a grimace.

She recalled every word Mickey Horton had said, every intonation, every "uppity" gesture. It was yet another instance of all the Hortons considering themselves to be so high and mighty compared to her—she was sure of it. And Kitty never forgot a real or imagined slight.

"Their time will come," she vowed.

There is nothing lonelier, Marie thought, than experiencing a loss and having no one to share it with. At the very moment Mark Brooks had discovered that he was Tommy Horton, Marie's world had come crashing down, leaving only horror and depression behind.

She had been in love with her own brother.

Marie trembled at the realization of how close they'd come to culminating the love she knew they both shared. And the feelings were still there, as deep and intense as ever.

Twice Tommy had called from the hospital. Marie had expected the first call but hadn't known what to say to him. It had been more of a silence than a conversation — there was really nothing she *could* say. They'd both agreed that it was fortunate no one else realized how . . . *important* she'd become to him — and he to her. Everyone believed she'd simply done a job to help Mark recover his memory. Nothing more.

Once her job had been completed, Marie had faded into the background. She'd accepted congratulations from Bill and avoided the family. The prospect of facing Kitty and of joining in any family celebrations was more than she could bear.

Tommy's second conversation was less awkward for him, but more awkward for Marie. He used their closeness to confide in her, to share all his qualms about Kitty. Finally she'd told him as gently as she could that she couldn't listen any more. He'd heard the tears in her voice as she'd begged him not to call again. Then in the long pause that followed, she could hear Tommy himself crying. The realization of what he was putting her through had overwhelmed him. They'd both said good-bye softly and then hung up. He hadn't called her again.

It was then that Marie began to feel as if she were losing her mind. It had been so different when Tony had died. Friends, family, even strangers had dropped by with cards, casseroles, and condolences. But there was no bereavement support for this kind of loss, no help whatsoever for a love that should never have happened. The sooner it was buried and forgotten, the better.

But the dreams persisted. Dreams in which she was walking hand in hand first with Tony, then with Mark Brooks, and finally with Tommy Horton. Sometimes the dreams went the other way—from Mark Brooks back to Tony. Each time, she woke up sobbing.

Every day she found herself awakening a little earlier than the day before. Soon she was waking up while it was still dark, trying without success to fall back asleep before morning. Finally convinced that she wouldn't be able to go back to sleep, she took to reading. Then as soon as it was light, but before anyone else was up, she began to take long walks through the quiet streets of Salem. The grass and trees still shimmered with early morning dew, and her footsteps echoed on the deserted pavement.

It was in this way that she first noticed a

small chapel set back from the street and approached by a winding path. However early Marie took her morning walk, there were always signs of life at the chapel. Some men in what looked like monk's robes were out cutting the shrubbery or tending the gardens. After a few days of each noticing the other, one monk began nodding to her. Then one day he gestured for her to enter the grounds, and she did. Since he smiled but did not speak, she wondered if he had taken a vow of silence. It didn't matter because it was pleasant sitting in the lovely garden and letting the peace and serenity flow through her like a refreshing cool breeze on a hot day.

Now Marie's nights didn't seem quite so desolate and interminable. She'd often heard the phrase, "the light at the end of the tunnel." For her, that light was a quiet, peaceful chapel garden in the hours before the city came to life.

But sadness and loneliness still clung to her like a shadow on a sunny day.

Then one day the little monk handed her a card. It read "If you should seek solace beyond that which is found in this garden, it may await you inside. Enter. You are welcome."

Chapter Seven

A Lifetime Guarantee

A pale, shaken, and exhausted Julie stepped off the plane at the Salem airport. When she couldn't spot her grandmother anywhere and then saw her uncle Mickey dash up to her, she didn't know whether to laugh or cry. Mickey quickly told her, "Whatever you're thinking is wrong. Calm down, little one. Your grandma wanted very much to come. As soon as your mother called her, Grandma's heart went out to you and she couldn't wait to cheer you up and help you plan for the future . . ."

"But . . ." Julie started.

"What do you mean?"

"What's the big 'but' that kept her away?"

"It's important to Grandma that you keep your privacy intact, and right now we have a very gossipy houseguest. We don't want to give her any more gossip fodder because her ear is connected to her mouth with no mind to separate them."

"Who in the world is that?" Julie demanded.

"Your sweet little aunt Kitty."

"Oh wow! What on earth is *she* doing here? I thought she hated all of us."

"Do I have a lot to fill you in on, little one!"

And he did. With the top down on the convertible to let in the fresh air and sunshine of a perfect day, Mickey and his niece, Julie, drove the hundred-plus miles out to Great-Aunt Martha's. Julie learned that currently around were an uncle Tommy she hardly remembered and an aunt Kitty she wished she could forget. And soon she would have another cousin. Mickey was as proud as could be when he told her he was an expectant father.

"What do you and Grandma think about me?" she asked in a serious tone after she'd congratulated him. "I know what I should do. I hoped that Momma could help me, but Daddy put an end to *that*, really quickly."

"Whatever you decide will be right for you. I know a lot of what you've been through, and for a girl your age you've behaved with remarkable maturity." Astonished, Julie turned around to look straight at Mickey. After the verbal battering she'd received from her father, she found it hard to believe that she was actually hearing a compliment. "Do you honestly mean that?"

"Of course I do. You have a fine mind and good instincts. I remember how you asked David to marry Susan in order to give her baby his name. I was there when Susan promised to release David. All of that is behind you now, but it made you grow up really fast."

"I'll never forgive Susan," Julie declared bitterly.

"Time takes care of a lot of those feelings, believe me."

When they arrived at Martha's, Julie almost felt as if she were back in Salem. Martha and her sister Alice looked alike and showed the same warmth and understanding. Martha insisted that Mickey stay for supper. And since Laura was out of town on a psychiatric consultation, he agreed.

Julie got right to the point. "Mother told me something about cousin Sally." When Martha nodded, Julie continued firmly, "Tell me about it, please. I have to know."

"Do you understand that this is entirely between us?" asked Martha. Julie nodded vigorously.

So Martha told Julie how her daughter had become pregnant while still in high school and had been sent to stay with relatives. After the baby was born, it had been put up for adoption. When Sally returned to town, nobody knew a thing about it. "It's not a secret from her husband, though," Martha added. "When she finally met Dan years later and decided to settle down, she insisted on telling him first. I'm proud to say that he loved her none the less for it."

"I always liked Dan," Julie concurred.

"But there's still no getting away from it.

Even in this day and age with girls wearing jeans and the freer atmosphere that rock and roll creates, you still have to consider your reputation. If you have a choice, it's better not to go parading around your hometown pregnant for nine months." Martha turned to Mickey and asked, "What do you say? Am I being too old-fashioned?"

"It's all a matter of perspective. Since this is still a new situation for Julie, and she has the opportunity of staying with you and enjoying the fresh country air, I'd say it's a good idea. At least for now. If she changes her mind and wants to parade around Salem at high noon stark naked, I'll meet her in court and put up bail for her."

Both women laughed. "Now that's what I'd call loyalty," said Martha, smiling.

"But there's more," Julie reminded her aunt. "What do I do once the baby's born?"

"You can keep it or put it up for adoption, as Sally did," Martha replied thoughtfully. "They were awfully nice folks, too, the ones who adopted the little girl. He was a pharmacist and she was a schoolteacher. They lived in —"

"You mean I get to see who the adopting parents are?" Julie interrupted excitedly, her eyes shining. "I can get to pick them, to give my okay? To make sure that they deserve my own little baby . . ." Suddenly Julie broke down, sobbing as if her heart were broken. She felt dreadfully embarrassed by her outburst and tried desperately to control herself. The conversation had been so practical, and she'd been treated just like an adult—Martha and Mickey had even shared adult confidences with her. And she had responded by crying like a child.

"There, there," Martha murmured gently. "You're just too tired right now, dear." Both Mickey and Martha marveled at how much stamina Julie had to have crossed the ocean twice in little more than two days and then to have driven all the way out to the farmland without complaint. Mickey kissed Julie good-bye and said he'd keep in touch, adding that Grandma Alice would drive out to visit within the next few days.

When Martha tucked her niece into the huge canopied brass bed, Julie felt safe for the first time in ages. "Get a good night's sleep, dear. We want to introduce you to a good local obstetrician. Then later, I'd like to drive you over to meet the Bannings."

"The *who*?" Julie mumbled, already half-asleep.

"The Bannings, dear," Martha repeated. "He's in the construction business and she's . . ." She looked down at Julie's fluttering eyelids. "Oh, you're too tired to talk about it now. But they're the sort of couple who would make wonderful parents. It's such a shame that they've never been able to have children in all these years. I really think you're going to take to them."

The day after Laura and Tom had their discussion, Laura received a message at the hospital asking her to arrange a meeting with Dr. Conrad at her convenience. Why do I think this has anything to do with my conversation with Tom Horton? she asked herself. She trusted that Tom, as he had promised, had not mentioned their discussion to anyone. Then she remembered something. Dr. Conrad was not only a close family friend of the Hortons', he was also Bill Horton's godfather.

The pathology department was located in the basement of Salem General, far away from the eyes of the public. There, autopsies were performed, biopsies examined and, occasionally, corpses identified. Laura arranged a meeting and, at the appointed time, left her sunny top-floor office and got in the elevator, feeling her heart sink as it descended to the basement.

Dr. Conrad met her at the elevator and led her briskly past a series of labs and the refrigerator room to his spacious, comfortable office. Perhaps to compensate for the lack of windows, he had several fine landscape murals on the walls and other colorful touches that somehow made Laura less uncomfortable.

"I called you here at the request of my godson." Laura, who had been sitting at the edge of her chair, tensed immediately. "No, please don't get up," Dr. Conrad added quickly. "I promise that this will be painless and quick. Bill is not here. I can pretty much guarantee that you will never see him alone again—unless you want to." When Laura remained poised, half-seated and half-standing, Dr. Conrad continued softly, "Please, Laura, trust me just this once." Slowly she seated herself again and allowed him to pour her a cup of coffee.

One look at Dr. Conrad's kindly eyes and warm, compassionate manner could win anyone over, Laura thought. It was a pity that most of the patients he came into contact with were dead—he was such a lively, charming fellow. She stirred her coffee, took a sip, and settled back to hear what he had to say.

"First of all, I want to assure you that I don't have the slightest idea what this is all about." He saw Laura's look of complete astonishment and added sincerely, "I mean every word of that. I have merely been chosen to be the messenger." He reached into the top drawer of his desk and pulled out a sealed envelope, placing it in the middle of his desk blotter. Laura looked at it as if it were some sort of dead animal.

Dr. Conrad waited for her to pick it up. When she didn't, he asked her to.

"Why should I?" she replied defensively. "You've already told me who it's from. That's all I need to know. There is nothing that Dr. William Horton has to say to me that I have any interest in hearing. As a matter of fact, this is all extremely childish. I can't imagine how you got roped into this."

Laura was immediately ashamed of herself for having lost control in front of Dr. Conrad. What had gotten into her? And how dare she speak that way to an older person and an important department head as well! She was relieved when he took it so calmly.

"That's a reasonable question, my dear. I am not normally a go-between. As I told Bill, this is both the first and last time I will ever get involved in something that is none of my business. When Bill first asked me, I said no. When he begged me, I said no. When he broke down and cried and said that other lives were involved, I agreed. I have known Bill all his life, and I do not ever recall seeing him cry. Ever. Frankly, I was impressed."

So was Laura. Tentatively she reached out for the envelope. "What's involved?" she asked cautiously.

"Bill simply wants me to sit here while you read whatever is inside so that I can assure him you have actually read it. He tells me that he's called you repeatedly and written to you, only to have his letters returned. He even thought of taping a message, but he was concerned that your secretary or someone else might hear it." He smiled at her. "Come on. What do you have to lose?"

Laura ripped open the envelope and read:

"What I did was criminal. I forced myself on you, assaulted you—yes, raped you, Laura. I am putting it all down on paper as a way of putting *my* life into *your* hands. I did it because I felt I had lost what was nearest and dearest to me—my right hand and the woman I love. I guess that's why. *You're* the shrink, not me. I flew into a rage greater than any I'd ever experienced before. But there is no excuse for what I did. I hereby promise you that I will never approach you again in my life. I will be polite at family gatherings. That's all. This letter is your guarantee. If I ever overstep myself again, simply expose this statement to the public. That will undoubtedly get me a well-deserved jail sentence and deprive me of a license to practice medicine.

"I am also aware that you can use the letter right now. The choice is yours. No punishment can relieve the feeling of guilt and horror I expect to carry to my grave."

The letter was dated and signed. Laura's eyes filled with tears as she read Bill's words. She was tempted to shred it and toss it in Dr. Conrad's wastebasket. Then she looked at the huge ashtray that Dr. Conrad used to accommodate his oversized cigars. She envisioned the words going up in smoke. Both were tempting ideas, but only for a fleeting second. Seeing Dr. Conrad seated, feet up, thumbing through a medical journal, she decided against doing either of these. She folded the letter, returned it to the envelope, and tucked it into her pocket. There would be plenty of time later to make decisions. Rising, she shook Dr. Conrad's hand, thanked him, and left.

Later on in the day, she began to feel an enormous sense of relief. For the first time she realized how much stress she'd been under. She and Bill were still working at the same hospital. Although she would never allow herself to be trapped by him again, he was still an ominous presence. Now that he'd acknowledged it directly and without excuses, she could breathe more easily.

It had been a late day. Although she should have waited for Tom to call, Laura wanted to share the contents of Bill's letter with him. She tried his office but got the answering service. When she called him at home, he answered on the second ring.

"How nice to hear from you," he said politely. "I'd just been thinking about our conversation the other night. I was planning to call you tomorrow morning."

Laura could tell from his tone of voice, and the fact that he did not call her by name, that Tom was not alone. But her newfound buoyancy urged her to continue. "You don't have to say anything," she told him, "but I can still talk from my end. I'm calling from my office and everyone's left for the day. I have a letter to read to you."

She proceeded to explain about her meeting with Dr. Conrad, then read him Bill's letter. She could tell, even from Tom's cautious response, that it meant a great deal to him. The difference between a pathological rapist and a disturbed man who admits his guilt and wants to atone for it was considerable, she knew—particularly to the man's father. "I hope you'll agree with me now that we mustn't tell Mickey about any of this," she added. "I hope this letter makes all the difference."

When they said good-bye and hung up, Laura felt sure that Tom would agree to let the whole incident drop. She sighed in relief.

A potentially explosive situation—one that had the power to destroy many lives—had been averted.

After Laura and Tom hung up, a third phone was carefully and silently replaced in its cradle.

"Can I use the phone, Mommy?" asked Sandy, suddenly appearing.

"Your grandfather's on the phone, you'll have to wait till he's finished."

"But you were—" Sandy didn't finish. Her mother had left the room and Sandy suddenly realized that this upstairs phone was an extension. She realized too that her mother was up to her old tricks again. She'd been fired before for eavesdropping, first when she was a receptionist, the second time she'd been working for a hotel. Sandy had wanted to call her father at the hospital and from now on would call him only when her mother was busy or out of the house. She had started telling him what life was like with Kitty. At first she'd been afraid that he would bawl her out for complaining about her own mother. When he'd seemed to understand and sympathize, she'd been so overwhelmed with gratitude that she'd cried.

As for Kitty, she returned to the privacy of her room with a look of triumph on her face. One single snatch of overheard conversation and she was on top of the world. She had a lot of grudges that dated back for years and she'd always been a scorekeeper. Now she gloated. Knowledge can be a weapon was her theory. When you know something that nobody else knows, it's an even bigger weapon. When you know something that only a few know and *they* don't know that *you* know, that's pure dynamite!

Long ago Kitty had learned to control herself when she felt this self-satisfied way. She had had to bide her time and make the right plans. She wanted to bring down the entire Horton family like a rack of bowling pins with a single strike. The higher and mightier they act, the harder they will fall, she told herself with a chuckle.

Bill had been very friendly toward "Mark" starting from their days in San Diego. And when Mark discovered that he was Bill's brother Tommy, the friendship had indeed deepened and the two brothers had become very close. Bill came frequently to Tommy's room to visit. When Tommy had learned that he had a spunky, affectionate, and very bright daughter, Bill had rejoiced with him. He'd also sympathized with Tommy about Kitty, and Tommy was grateful for his brother's support and concern.

Bill had no idea what Tommy had ever seen in that woman. Perhaps she had once been pretty, though in a common, vapid way, when she was a young woman. But even as a young woman, her tongue had been as sharp as her nose.

Tommy told Bill how he'd met Kitty on a blind date when she'd been staying with a friend in Salem. She lived in a small mill town upstate, and after that first date, they'd begun to visit each other's hometowns regularly. As soon as Tommy had been drafted, they'd gotten married, and soon afterward he'd been sent to Korea. But the bitter, small-minded, gossipy woman who greeted him when his memory had returned was more of a stranger than anyone he'd met during his amnesia.

Mickey had called Bill several days earlier to recount his own run-in with Kitty. "I'm no doctor," he said, "but even a layman can see that worrying him to death about the competency of the hospital and the surgeons, questioning him disapprovingly about every procedure, and predicting the worst isn't going to help Tommy recover."

The two brothers had agreed that there was little they could do but remember Mickey's warning and keep an eye on Tommy.

Sometimes while wondering what he could do, Bill Horton thought of all the sports in which there were specialized participants. He thought of baseball with its *designated hitters,* the home-run champs of whom little else was expected. But that wouldn't apply to him, he decided. Ever since he'd been named administrative head of surgery, he'd looked for parallels in other fields—other specialized participants. He had surgeons and plastic surgeons under his supervision, each of whom looked to him for some sort of guidance, even if it was just to reschedule something or change an operating room scrub team. And each of them had what he no longer had—the supple dexterity to successfully perform an operation.

He thought of rowing and the fellow who sits in the rear of a shell, yelling out instructions to the rowing team through a megaphone. One day he mentioned this to Tommy when he dropped in for one of his many visits.

"Look at you!" Tommy had retorted. "Do you know what a coxswain looks like? In order not to weigh the boat down, they try to pick a fellow who's ninety-five pounds wringing wet."

Bill was a strapping six foot two.

And he had noble, clean-cut features. More than half of the women at Salem General would have given anything for him to notice them—in a romantic way. Men would look at him and think that a man like that could have as many women as he wanted, any time, any place. And people who knew him said that Bill Horton had charisma.

Lying in the hospital, Tommy had a great deal of time to think as he recovered from one graft and prepared for the next. Bill always took pains to explain each procedure to him. And while Tommy listened to his brother, staring at the face before him, he thought, *That's* what I want to look like!

The old Tommy would have felt much too awkward to mention such a thing. But now he felt more than comfortable with Bill.

"How much of a choice do I have?" Tommy asked. "I mean, it isn't every day that a fellow is given the chance to pick out a new face."

And because Tommy had phrased it lightly so that it would be taken as a joke, Bill obliged him by laughing. "It's not that simple, you old clown," he replied affectionately. "We're surgeons, not magicians."

But Tommy pressed on. "Seriously, Bill. I've heard of the remarkable changes you and your staff have brought about."

"Within prescribed limitations," Bill pointed out carefully.

"But you're giving me an entirely new jaw," Tommy protested.

"Good old Tommy! There you go again, exaggerating just the way you used to when we were kids. It was only a *portion* of the jaw, an inch here, an inch and a half there." Bill could see that Tommy was disappointed. He leaned forward and tried to explain why his brother couldn't have the face of his choice. But it was extremely difficult for a nonmedical person to understand something so complicated. Suddenly he had an idea.

"Do you remember how I took all those measurements and began sketching you when you were still receiving burn treatment in California?" Tommy nodded. "A day or two ago I ran across those sketches in my files. I hadn't referred to them for a while, because once we discovered who you were, I had plenty of snapshots to guide me. Well, I compared the composite sketch we made here with the ones I'd made on the Coast when I didn't know who you were. And guess what?"

Tommy shrugged. "One looked like the other. But why?"

"Because in a well-built, well-arranged face like yours, with clear-cut, even features, everything falls into balance. A little more height in the cheekbones, a stronger jut to the chin, a wider jawline, and you'd look lopsided. I *know* you wouldn't want *that!*" He punched his brother playfully but gently on the shoulder. Tommy smiled and looked up at him.

"You were a pretty classy-looking guy, you know. If we can make you look anywhere nearly as good as you looked going *into* the war, I'll feel it is a job well done."

"*Can* you?" a voice demanded from the door. Both men looked up to see Kitty approaching. There was no telling how long she'd stood there until she opened her mouth again. "'*If* we can,' is what *you* say. I don't want there to be any 'ifs' about it. Either you're sure, or let someone who knows what he's doing finish the job."

Out of the corner of his eye, Bill saw Tommy tense up. He patted his brother's hand to reassure him, then pushed the buzzer and turned, smiling, to his sister-in-law. He was grateful to Mickey for having forewarned him. "Hello, Kitty. I was in the midst of making my rounds, visiting my patients." A nurse looked in and Bill said firmly, "Would you please show Mrs. Horton to the visitors' lounge and get her a cup of coffee? I haven't completed examining and evaluating her husband."

Kitty was led by her arm down the hall, still gaping with astonishment.

As soon as she'd left, Tommy's eyes brimmed with tears. Seeing this, Bill said gently, "One of the problems of long-term surgery is that it depletes your energy. When that happens, you can get wiped out for no reason at all. It's like the flu, when you feel so weak, you could cry." Tommy nodded, not trusting himself to speak. "Don't worry about what Kitty said. I require only that the patient believe in my medical ability and good judgment. If we had to take a poll of relatives, no doctor could stay in business for long."

Tommy smiled at his brother in gratitude. "She didn't really mean it. It's just that she's—"

"You leave that up to me," Bill replied briskly. "You look tired. Would you like me to tell her to come back later so that you can take a nap?"

Tommy shook his head and squared his shoulders manfully, looking as if he were ready to swallow a necessary but very bitter pill. He had to see her sooner or later—and it might as well be sooner.

Kitty sat in the pleasant fourth-floor visitors' alcove, tapping her foot impatiently. She was certain that Bill had sent her out of the room just to demonstrate his power as a big-shot doctor. She was equally certain that he was filling her husband's mind with nasty ideas about her. Those Horton men stuck together like glue. That's why she was eager to get Tommy upstate again, away from their influence. She did not realize that everything she attributed to them was exactly what she herself thought and did.

Out of the corner of her eye, Kitty watched Bill leave Tommy's room and walk down the long corridor in her direction. She screwed up her face in distaste as she observed the sureness of his stride, the way he held his handsome blond head high and smiled at the nurses he passed.

"I'm finished now, if you'd like to go in," he said politely, smiling at Kitty. "While I'm here, if there's any procedure that we're doing that puzzles or bothers you, I'd be happy to answer any questions you may have."

"No thank you," she replied with more emphasis than seemed necessary.

Bill accompanied her back down the hall. "He seems a bit tired, so I suggest you don't stay too long."

Kitty marveled at the smile Bill seemed to have pasted on his face. Whatever she said, whatever tone of voice she used, nothing seemed to faze him.

"I'm still his wife, you know."

"And I'm still his doctor," Bill answered pleasantly as they parted outside Tommy's room.

Later as Kitty drove away from the hospital, she had an eerie smile on her face.

Had Sandy been there to spot it, she would have known to stay out of her mother's way, that something unpleasant was about to occur. Kitty had been trying to decide which of Tommy's brothers she hated the most. She was winding up for a confrontation with that brother in which she would make the strongest accusations she could, then sit back and watch the fur fly. A few days ago she would have picked Mickey. The way he'd talked to her as if she were a child and he a teacher had rankled her deeply and for a long time. But now she decided that Bill's attitude was even more insufferable, and her eyes narrowed spitefully. What she wouldn't give to wipe that smirk off his mouth!

Suddenly Kitty stopped the car by the side of the road and leaned her head on the wheel. There were those palpitations again. She reached for a nitroglycerine tablet and placed it under her tongue, resolving to take a good long nap when she got home. One of these days she intended to shout the wrath of heaven down on all the Hortons. And she didn't want to have to gasp for breath or have one of those fainting spells right in the middle of it.

Feeling better after a short rest, Kitty started the car and drove away. Once more that eerie smile distorted her features as she envisioned the upcoming confrontation.

It would be her finest hour, she resolved, and it was well worth waiting for.

Chapter Eight

Fear of the Past

Marie continued to visit the chapel garden for several mornings before she ever considered entering the building itself. The day the little monk had approached and handed her the printed note, her hand had trembled as she'd read the invitation. It had been ages since she'd spoken face to face with anyone. She'd only had phone conversations and kept them brief, acclimating herself slowly to loneliness until now it seemed like an old friend.

She knew if she went inside the building and had to talk with anyone, she wouldn't be able to cope with it. Just the *thought* of having to communicate with anyone filled her with apprehension, agitation, and fear.

Although she herself did not realize, Marie had changed a great deal in the past weeks—and not just emotionally. The restless days and sleepless nights had taken their toll on her body. She had lost a considerable amount of weight, which had sharpened her soft features, and her eyes were ringed with dark shadows that looked like bruises. She now walked with her head bent over hunched shoulders, like some careworn peasant carrying all her belongings on her back.

Another day the monk handed her another card. "The faith-giving power of understanding can see past differences to universality. Forgive yourself and let the illuminating power of love heal hurt feelings, mistakes of the past, regrets, and recriminations."

This time, Marie's hand did not tremble as she held and read the note. She thanked the monk, put the card in her pocket, and approached the chapel. Once she crossed the threshold, her pace quickened. Sunlight filtered through the stained-glass windows, creating brilliant patterns on the floor. From the shadows, a voice rang out.

"Welcome, my child. I'm so glad that you decided to visit. I'm Father John."

As Marie's eyes got used to the dimmer inside she made out a tall, thin man with a kindly, gentle face. She followed him past rows of benches to a room off to one side which might have been designed during the Middle Ages. There were high-backed benches, three-legged stools, and a high-standing writing table. Two of the walls were almost all window. Marie watched the bright colors dance across Father John's robe as they sat down.

"You can tell me whatever you like, my

child," he said gently. "Nothing will ever go beyond this room. Here you will always be safe, as will all your thoughts, dreams, and fears."

And so it was that Marie finally unburdened herself to Father John. The words tumbled out one after the other, sometimes in the wrong order. Anyone else might have gotten confused trying to sort out all the family members and relationships among them, but Father John heard her with a sympathetic, comprehending spirit.

What Marie had perceived as cowardliness and confusion on her part, Father John knew to be courage. What she found hopelessly muddled, he explained clearly. And when, after having relived so much that was emotionally wrenching, she grew too tired to go on, Father John suggested that they stop and continue another day.

On Marie's third visit she tentatively broached the subject of her future. Up until then, it had been impossible to plan beyond the next sleepless night. "Could you help me enter a convent?" she asked shyly.

Father John told her that such decisions were not so easily made, that she must be sure that is what she really wanted to do.

By Marie's fifth visit, Father John was convinced that she would do well in their order's convent. He realized that she had been neglecting her health, often forgetting to eat from one day to the next. She was growing frail and might fall seriously ill. Father John told himself that Marie needed to be surrounded by those who were aware of her condition and who would care about her and for her. He deeply felt that life was precious and that people needed to be at peace with themselves, not suffer undeserved and unnecessary anguish.

The next day Marie arrived at the chapel grounds with a small overnight bag. She hadn't told her family or any friends for fear they would try to stop her or talk her out of her decision. Instead, she'd written a letter to her parents, which she asked Father John to mail for her.

It was a long drive to the convent. The little monk who tended the garden gave her a sack of apples, some cheese, and a long loaf of homemade bread. Another monk sat at the wheel of an old but well-tended sedan. By the time the car pulled away, Marie's eyes were growing lively, glowing with anticipation. An hour out of town, she opened the paper sack and ate an apple. It was the first food she'd actually *tasted* in longer than she could remember, and she enjoyed every bite. Then before long she finished all the cheese and half of the loaf of bread. The weight of the past was being lifted from her shoulders.

Tommy was back in the hospital, undergoing the second day of a three-day procedure. Again and again the plastic surgery team had cautioned him to be patient. This time they needed to "harvest" bone cartilage.

Tommy winced at the term. "Harvest?" he asked them. "Do I look like some sort of farm to you? If I do, why don't you knock me out, pick up your shovels and rakes and wheelbarrows, and take all you need. Just wake me up when it's over."

Of course, it wasn't that simple, and he tried to be patient. But Kitty had been nagging at him again, about how the hospital was dragging everything out in order to "build up" the medical expenses. Kitty felt that all people had hidden motives for their actions, and it was up to her to expose them.

She was still raving when Bill Horton dropped in. Funny how often his visits coincide with mine, thought Kitty. Once again he gave her the broad, bland smile that infuriated her, then he waved and began walking down the hall before she could react.

Kitty was just furious. She tried to call after Bill but found herself short of breath. With an effort, she ran out of Tommy's room and down the hall, toward the big horseshoe counter that served as the nurses' station. Bill was there, chatting with one of the nurses and there were some orderlies sipping coffee.

Kitty came up to Bill and began screaming.

"I know that you've sired a bastard haven't you, Dr. Horton? You womanizer. You . . ." As a string of curse words echoed through the corridors, nurses, orderlies, and a passing doctor looked at Bill questioningly.

He waved them away. By now he was convinced the woman was stark raving mad. He hadn't the slightest idea what "bastard" she was talking about or what she meant by "womanizing." For a quick instant he thought she might have interpreted his smiles as a form of flirtation.

The medical personnel now realized this was a family matter and out of deference to Bill gave the ugly scene as wide a berth as they could. Kitty would have none of it. She shrieked to them to "listen to what kind of whoremaster and hypocrite Bill was." They were all utterly shocked and they remained frozen in place some distance away.

"What the hell are you talking about, Kitty?" Bill asked sharply. "Do you realize what a scene you're making?"

"Not like you, huh?" she sneered. "You like to work behind the scenes, screwing your sweet little sister-in-law. *You're* the father of her baby you know."

Bill's eyes widened as his thoughts raced. He wondered where Kitty had got her information. Had it been from the letter he'd sent to Laura? He grabbed Kitty by the shoulders and, for the record, stated firmly, "You've got things confused. Mickey is the baby's father. Mickey is Laura's husband."

Kitty's sneer blossomed into an evil-looking grimace of triumph. "Mickey is sterile. Your father gave him a test and he's sterile. I heard Laura talking with your father over the phone. Mickey doesn't know yet, but I promise you he will!"

Dumbfounded and devastated by the damage this woman was capable of doing, Bill began to shake her like a man possessed. "Stop it! Stop it right now! You don't know what you're saying."

Then all of a sudden he felt Kitty slip from his grip. The hand that had been clutching her shoulders was now suspended in empty air. Instinctively, however, he was able to break her fall and catch her before she hit the floor.

The secluded Banning farm overlooking Lake Plunkett offered an idyllic setting for the raising of happy, healthy children. Every time Julie visited there she realized more and more that it was a perfect place for a child to grow up.

When Julie had been a first grader, Salem residents still referred to the area as "way out in the country." But urban sprawl had so expanded the city proper that the Banning farm was now formally listed on the tax rolls as being within one of the newer suburbs.

"But as you can see, that's just to satisfy city regulations," Scott Banning said, gesturing expansively at the unspoiled vista before them.

Scott Banning was a stocky, compactly built, sandy-haired man in his early thirties. The day Julie met him, he'd been wearing a bright plaid cotton shirt, neatly pressed chinos, and penny loafers. At first she'd thought that these were his weekend clothes, but his wife, Janet, had laughed when she'd commented on it. "This is about as dressed up as Scott ever gets," she'd told Julie, smiling. "Unless there's some big 'do' in the city and then I wear my heels and he wears his vested blue serge suit."

This appealed to Julie. Living with the Bannings would be a good, healthy life for a child. As she sat thinking about this on the roomy back porch swing, Julie relaxed and stretched her legs. Now that she was so far along in her pregnancy, she could barely see over her stomach to her sandals.

Again and again Julie told herself that her Great-Aunt Martha was absolutely right. She had to take care of herself in order to bring a healthy baby into the world—and she also had to plan ahead. Long conversations with both Great-Aunt Martha and Grandma Alice had convinced her to put the baby up for adoption. As Alice had pointed out, Julie was still a teenager herself and had barely begun to live. How could she possibly take care of herself *and* be both mother and father to her child? The prospect was overwhelming.

Fortunately Martha had been able to put her in touch with the ideal parents. Scott and Janet Banning who had been childless for years were presently on the lists of several adoption agencies. "Way far down on the lists," Janet had added with a mixture of longing and frustration. The several times Julie had visited Scott and Janet's home had confirmed her initial impression. They were the sort of parents *she* would have wanted.

As a general building contractor, Scott was nowhere near as wealthy as Ben Olson, but that was fine with Julie. Her father had lots of drive and ambition, he'd scratched and clawed his way up from being a small-town banker to international financier. But he was cold, calculating, and incapable of love or affection. Ben would never consider stopping along the road to bird-watch or hunt for a four-leaf clover. But Scott would and did.

Fishing was high on Scott's list, and he longed to teach a son or daughter how to sail. With Lake Plunkett a stone's throw away, nothing would be easier. It was now only a matter of time.

"And of course ice skating in the winter when the lake freezes over," added Janet. "We all love that around here,"

Janet was a schoolteacher but planned to retire when they adopted a baby. "I'm in a holding pattern," she told Julie. I long for the day when I teach just one child at a time."

Julie thought of her own mother, ready to fly away at a moment's notice, leaving her children to fend for themselves in a house full of indifferent servants. It wasn't so much that Addie *chose* to leave her children; it was more that she never dared cross her husband. He was an autocrat who expected his family to snap to attention just as his employees did. "It was if he 'fired me' when I broke the rules and got pregnant," Julie observed ruefully to Martha.

Two of the first things Julie had looked for in Janet Banning were spunk and character. And Julie had concluded that she had them in great abundance. She'd firmly resisted tempting offers to adopt black market babies because she disapproved of anything shady or unfair. She made no promises she couldn't keep. *She* was the one with the inner strength to hold a family together, inspire the best in people, teach loyalty, morality, and—most of all—love.

Julie finished sipping her lemonade and gazed at the spacious, emerald green lawn overlooking the lake. Trees in full leaf circled an area just right for a game of tag; she envisioned softball games and children tumbling on the grass or cavorting in a treehouse. It would be indeed a good life for her child.

She got up carefully, hefting the extra weight, and said her good-byes. Scott and Janet walked her out to the car. They all promised to keep in touch now that her "time" was approaching. A smiling, relaxed Julie drove back to Martha's, her mind completely at ease. Maybe some things in life *do* turn out for the best, she began to realize.

Currently, all her thoughts centered on that tiny being kicking energetically inside her. She had been reading a good deal about pregnancy and child care and comparing it with what she'd learned on her own. A baby, she realized, needed special care as well from the moment it left the safety of the womb. She herself could have felt a lot more secure if she'd had a really caring mother.

Janet Banning would be a really caring mother—someone a child could turn to and rely on for warmth, protection, cuddling, and endless love. Scott too, she felt, would doubtlessly be a wonderful father. But when Julie had finally agreed to give her baby to the Bannings, it was primarily because of Janet.

Chapter Nine

Joy for the Future

Usually when a cardiac emergency or a stroke occurs, a phone call has to be made and an ambulance sent. Since Kitty collapsed right in Salem General Hospital, precious minutes were saved and in no time she was in the emergency room. Even as she was positioned on the litter, a tube was placed in her mouth to help her breathe, and oxygen was administered before the elevator doors closed.

Bill stayed behind, stunned and certain he would merely be in the way. He shuddered to picture exactly what the doctors would be doing—starting an intravenous line, placing Kitty on a cardiac monitor . . .

Nurse Grant, who had been supervising the fourth floor all afternoon, looked at Bill with compassion and asked if there was anything she could do. Without looking up, he answered, "Please call my father. He'll know what to say to Tommy."

Once a patient is stabilized, the doctors usually ask for a complete medical history. In this case, because Kitty wasn't able to speak, a young resident was sent to question Tommy. He could tell them nothing about his wife's previous "condition," however. She'd been perfectly healthy when they had been together, and since their reunion, she had mentioned nothing to the contrary. The resident went through the list on his clipboard. Pencil poised, he rattled off, "No periods of unconsciousness? Headaches? Seizure? Prior strokes? Heart attack? Hypertension? What about—"

"No! No! No, I tell you. I don't know a damn thing. Kitty has always been a hypochondriac. I'm sure if there were anything wrong, she would have told me over and over and over again."

Tom Horton entered his son's room in the midst of this highly charged interrogation. The resident recognized him and stopped the questioning. Tom went over to his son's bedside and put a comforting hand on his shoulder.

The resident, frustrated at having been interrupted, walked over to the window. There, sitting on the ledge, was the handbag Kitty had left when she'd run out into the hall to confront Bill. Unnoticed, he opened it and began to rummage through it.

Tommy asked his father to tell the resident to go, adding, "There is or was, nothing wrong with Kitty."

"Oh no?" said the resident with a note of

triumph in his voice. "Then what's she been using *this* for?" The bottle he held up contained her nitroglycerine tablets, and the instructions read, "Place one under the tongue when needed."

Later, when they had managed to track down the upstate doctor whose name was on the bottle label, he told them he had been treating her for a heart condition over the past four years. "She has been courting a heart attack or stroke for years. She has hypertension and is greatly excitable. This is a small town, Doctor, and I can assure you that Kitty Horton lost many jobs because of her temper. I kept telling her that she could always get another job, but she couldn't get a new heart. I tried sedatives, tranquilizers, everything I could think of to get her to relax. I urged her to change her life-style, to lower those risk factors. But there was always that terrible temper." The doctor paused, wondering whether he'd said too much, but then remembered after all, he was speaking with a colleague. "Is that what happened this time?" he asked curiously. "Did she lose her temper?"

The resident checked his notes. "I wasn't right there sir, but you could sure hear her all over the floor. Sounded like a whole lot of threats and cursing, you know."

The upstate doctor knew only too well. He would have given up on Kitty long ago if it hadn't been for her little girl, Sandy.

Then within a couple of hours after having been taken to the emergency room, Kitty was dead. The doctors called it an "acute cerebral hemorrhage with massive complications." They had tried to resuscitate her several times by electrically stimulating her heart. But finally the monitor had registered brain death. Nothing responded.

Tom Horton now had two sons to comfort. After doing his best to say some kind words about Kitty to Tommy, he left him with Alice, who promised to stay until lights out.

Tom found Bill in his office with all the lights off. He was staring out the window as little beads of rain ran in rivulets down the pane. Far below he could faintly hear the sirens of ambulances careening around the corner and into the emergency entrance. He knew that doors were being opened for stretchers to be wheeled out. Below, all was frenzied action. Above, all was quiet as Bill stood frozen in profile by the window.

At the sound of his father's voice, he turned around. "I got the word about a half hour ago. I assume that they tried everything; they always do. I guess we're all pretty good at our job here—" Bill's voice broke, and he sat on the desk, head in hand. "Boy," he sobbed, "leave it to me, huh?"

"It was an accident, son," Tom said gently. "A cerebral accident."

Bill shook his head vigorously. "I don't care what they say in pathology. Whatever they call it, I did it. I lost my temper and shook her to death."

Tom grabbed Bill by the shoulders and said firmly, "Stop saying that this minute.

Someone may overhear you."

Bill lifted his head to his father with a grim look. What a ridiculous thing to say, he thought. A full floor of dependable, dedicated personnel had been present during Kitty's little scene. She couldn't have timed it better if she'd tried. Perhaps that's exactly what she'd had in mind all along, he conjectured, the way she ran out of Tommy's room and picked the most crowded area around for her explosion.

Tom had just turned the lights on so that he could see his son better, when there was a rap on the door. The two men who stood on the threshold identified themselves as precinct police officers.

"Dr. Horton?" they asked. When both father and son nodded, they consulted their notes. "Dr. *William* Horton?"

"That's me, Officer. How can I help you?"

Before Bill could reply, Mickey strode in, looking vigorous, natty, and alert, particularly compared with his father and brother. He and the policemen greeted one another in a friendly, familiar manner. Although Mickey no longer frequented the courthouse and police station as he had in the early days of his practice, he was still in touch.

"I'm sure this is all a formality, isn't it?" he asked them with more confidence than he felt. "You fellows know my brother's reputation as a surgeon, don't you?"

They both nodded. Neither man had to be told that this was top-level stuff. Both would have preferred to have been frisking an armed robber or picking up a speeder. But the choice was not theirs.

"You know how it is," they said to Mickey. "The lady gets shook up and then drops dead. It's not up to us to make the connection. We just have to bring him in."

"Were there witnesses?" Mickey asked. Then he caught the expression in Bill's eyes and knew without having to ask further that there must have been enough witnesses to fill a courtroom.

"All right," Mickey agreed with a practiced smile, looking at Bill. "This shouldn't take long. They just want to take you down in front of a judge who will instruct you to make yourself available for the next few weeks or months." He then grinned at Bill. "No sweat. You should be home in a couple of hours." Next to no one in particular, he said, "Mind if I accompany you?" and tagged along to the precinct house.

Bill had plenty of time to think on the drive down to the police station. Until today two people—his father and Laura—had thought that they shared a secret. If Kitty hadn't eavesdropped, nobody else, least of all himself, would know that Laura was carrying his child. As far as he knew, Tom and Laura still considered it their secret. And if it were up to him, he'd leave it that way. But it all depended upon what had been overheard.

When Bill gave it more thought, he was certain Kitty had deliberately chosen the time and place to broadcast what she'd learned in order to harm as many innocent people as she could. Salem General Hospital was practically home to a good part of the Horton family. She must have realized that with one vicious stroke she could practically wipe them all out.

He hoped against hope that there was still a chance her accusations had not been overheard. He remembered that the staff had deliberately moved out of earshot at one point. But when?

It was clear to Bill that he'd find out soon enough. Everyone who had been present would be questioned. Until then, he could only wonder.

Whatever happened, he would refuse Mickey's offer to defend him. The man's shrewdness, intelligence, and legal acumen were beyond reproach; he could find no one better. But Mickey was a brother he had betrayed. He had raped this brother's wife— was father to the child that would bear his brother's name. He would never be able to apologize to Mickey for that. Indeed, he could never say anything about it at all. Tom and Laura had decided never to reveal the child's true paternity. He too would keep that secret— to the grave, if need be. If only other's hadn't heard it.

As the patrol car turned into the precinct parking lot, Bill made up his mind. He knew where he stood and what he would have to tell Mickey. He recalled an old saying—"Three people may keep a secret, if two of them are dead." Bill reflected that one person had already died tonight. If a second had to die . . . it would not be his father or his sister-in-law, Laura.

* * *

It was lights-out time at the hospital. At Alice's insistence, one of the nurses called in a surgeon who was part of Bill's team to check a graft that seemed to be irritating Tommy. It was inspected and the bandages were readjusted. The next day if all the stitches stayed in place and the skin grafts looked pink and uninfected, Tommy was due to be released.

When the surgeon had finished, Alice kissed her son good night and left him looking like a forlorn little boy, covered in bandages and miserable. And although they had given Tommy something to sleep, he kept waking up. All night and through most of the next day, the phone at Marie's little cottage kept ringing. But it remained unanswered.

Julie was not present when her baby was handed over to Scott and Janet Banning. The birth itself was easy and unremarkable—after a brief labor, she was delivered of a ten-pound baby boy. Later she had them bring him in to her room for a brief visit before giving him up for good. She kissed his ten little fingers and ten tiny toes, held him close to her, then handed him back to the nurse without a word.

Presumably, Julie surmised, the Bannings were waiting downstairs to see the baby and make arrangements to transport him back to their home. Previously she had delighted in their anticipation of her child. The depth of their longing and, later, the gratitude over her decision had been constantly reassuring to her. But at this point she didn't trust herself to be gracious, or even civilized. The "maternal instinct" she had often heard about was consuming her. She closed the door to her hospital room and started fiddling with the dial on the TV set. After a while she slept.

Later when she was back at Martha's, Julie was able to see things with a clearer perspective. A note awaited her from Grandma Alice, that said, "You have the rest of your life ahead of you. May it be a wonderful life. All my love."

When she showed it to Martha, her great-aunt said, "It's true, you know. That's why my sister thought of sending you here. Nobody knows your business. You have nobody at home to explain to or apologize to—unless you want to. Because you've kept away from Salem, the slate for all intents and purposes is wiped clean."

"Not for me, Aunt Martha," Julie answered, sighing heavily. "I'll never forget that I had a son and gave him away."

"Do you feel you made the best choice you could under the circumstances?"

"Yes, Aunt Martha."

"Are you certain in your heart about Scott and Janet Banning?"

"Yes, Aunt Martha. It's just that . . . well . . . it doesn't seem fair."

Her great-aunt reminded her that the late President John Kennedy had once observed that life wasn't fair. She took Julie's young head in her gnarled hands, looked into her eyes, and said, "But we all persevere. We do the best we can. Sally did. And you will, too."

"You think so?" Julie asked hopefully.

"I *know* so. I feel it in my bones, and believe me, these old bones have felt a lot and ought to know a lot by now."

It was a time for new beginnings, a time to carve out a fresh life. Julie decided to get back in shape before returning to Salem. Friends and neighbors knew that she had gone to Europe to visit her parents, and since then, if anyone inquired after her, her grandparents had merely said that she was "away" or "visiting." But now, as she looked at her figure in the mirror, Julie realized she had a lot of work to do on herself. Then she thought, How about a gorgeous tan to go with a svelte shape?

Using her charge card, she dialed Palm Beach, Florida, information, then called her longtime friend and confidante, Alva Hurtado.

The Hurtados were one of the most distinguished families in that ultrafancy, well-patrolled island community of millionaires—except in the eyes of their lonely, adventurous daughter, Alva. Julie had met Alva on the beach one day when both girls had been feeling put-upon by their parents. They'd exchanged confidences as ten-year-old tomboys and Christmas cards and birthday cards ever since. Julie had flown to Caracas for Alva's first wedding. Now twice divorced, Alva often invited Julie to Palm Beach for a visit.

Had Julie called one day earlier, she would have missed Alva. Her friend had just returned from a long tour through Europe to the Far East, Hong Kong, Hawaii, and back home again. She was delighted to hear from Julie and said she had lots to tell her.

"I have lots to tell you, too . . . but I'd rather tell you about it in person," Julie said.

"You're coming down? Marvelous! I am going to line up dozens of cute men for you to meet. Do you speak Italian yet? Spanish? You have your pick. Even Americans!"

Julie calmed her friend down and suggested that no plans be made until she arrived. She would need a week or two of rest, recuperation, and tanning before getting into the social scene.

"No problem," Alva reassured her cheerfully. "I will place my hairdresser on call. You know how secluded our own beach is. And guess what?" She giggled. "I have just put in my own gymnasium. All the walls are mirrored. If that doesn't get you back in shape, nothing will."

Aunt Sally and Uncle Dan drove Julie to the airport. Julie had decided that the few clothes she had would suit her when she first arrived in Palm Beach. She and Alva were pretty much the same size. Later, when she got into shape, there was all of Worth Avenue to visit—shops that were the envy of the rest of the smart world.

Once aboard the plane, with a complimentary glass of wine in her hand, Julie found herself looking forward to the future. The last thing Alva had said was, "We will have a lot of catching up to do, no?"

Yes, Julie thought, they would. But only on the first day. From then on, it was straight into whatever lay ahead.

Chapter Ten
The Best Defense

When blue-eyed Michael Horton entered the world at a strapping nine pounds (which Mickey called "all muscle"), the entire Horton family celebrated the joyous occasion.

Julie sent a telegram and flowers from Palm Beach, followed by a sterling silver baby cup from a fancy shop on Worth Avenue. "Even the wrapping paper looks like sterling silver," Sandy Horton observed when she was watching Laura unwrap it.

Neither Tommy nor his daughter, Sandy, visited Laura at the hospital. Everyone understood, of course, especially Laura. After all, he'd undergone a number of painful operations there—and his wife had died there.

"I only hope that Kitty's death, having come so suddenly and violently, doesn't create any posttraumatic stress disorders," she confided to Mickey. Psychologists had been discovering these disorders in Korean and Vietnam veterans, she explained. Even some World War II prisoners of war and concentration-camp inmates were still suffering from them.

Mickey had been reading some of his wife's textbooks on psychiatry, trying to familiarize himself with the subject. In many of his criminal court cases, he was forced to deal with conflicting psychiatric testimony. Now that it was possible that his brother Tommy might have some kind of new psychological problem, he was even more interested than ever. He asked Laura to explain further.

"Not *new*, dear. People who suffer this stress disorder are merely regressing, reliving dreadful past experiences. They may have trouble sleeping and concentrating on things. Some have frequent nightmares and disturbing thoughts. Many are frightened of loud noises and, because of all they have lost, are afraid of forming any emotional attachments."

Both Laura and Mickey realized that this last was not one of Tommy's symptoms. He welcomed all the love and reassurance the family could give him, and he and little Sandy were almost inseparable. His parents and daughter had accompanied him upstate for the funeral and burial. Kitty owned a plot next to that of her parents and had always expressed a wish to be buried in her hometown.

The local pastor had barely known her, and the little he'd heard was not at all encouraging for a proper eulogy. He waited until he'd met the husband, daughter, and in-laws, who so impressed him with their sincerity and decency that he decided to speak of "the family" and thus, by implication, Kitty. Very few nonfamily people attended. Those who did came more out of curiosity than out of friendship. No one who had known Kitty had liked her—she'd made that impossible.

When the funeral was over, Tommy and Sandy returned to the big white colonial corner house in Salem that generations of Hortons had called home.

Next to the baby's parents, the one most excited about little Michael was Sandy. She wanted to learn everything, help with everything, hold the baby, and play with him. From a frightened, neglected child who'd managed to survive a dreary, emotionally harrowing life with her mother, Sandy was blossoming into a beautiful young lady under the love of a new father and doting family.

"Why does the baby have blue eyes?" she asked her grandfather.

"Most babies that age do," Tom answered, smiling.

"Will they change later? What color will they be?"

Here Tom was on safe ground. All of his sons had hazel eyes and Laura's were green. But as he spoke to Sandy, his thoughts touched briefly on the baby's true parentage. He was thankful now that he'd decided not to reveal Laura's secret—the truth about the rape would certainly have caused Bill to lose his license to practice medicine, and incurred a jail sentence.

But how different was it now? Tom sadly

wondered. Bill would soon be on trial anyway. A prison sentence loomed before him and, with it, the loss of his license as well. Tom was convinced Kitty's death had been an accident, certain that Bill had not known about her heart condition. In fact, nobody in Salem had known, including her own husband.

As Tom considered how gloomy things looked, one bright spot emerged. Mickey and Laura were thrilled with the baby. The family as a unit was at peace. It almost seemed as though Kitty's death had brought them all even closer together than before.

Tommy's family loyalty had also stood the test of this tragedy. Many times since his return, he had longed to shake some sense into Kitty. How well he remembered having done that early in their marriage before he'd been sent to Korea. He had no idea what she'd said to Bill, but he knew Kitty had been able to set anyone's teeth on edge. He wondered if she'd been bad-mouthing him, if Bill had simply been defending his brother's honor. It made sense. He would have done the same.

Tommy mourned Kitty. But not too much.

Tom, Tommy, and Mickey each tried in his own way to deal with one big question: What had Bill and Kitty been arguing about?

About one thing Mickey was very bemused and sad. At home he had a wife and a bouncing baby boy to delight him. At the office he had enough legal cases to keep two secretaries and a clerk busy for months—he certainly didn't need any new business. But the one client he wanted desperately to take on did not want him. Bill had refused his services.

He knew very well that had he been able to take Bill's case, he could never have handled his regular practice. Nevertheless, he was deeply hurt by Bill's rejection. What other lawyer knew Bill and Kitty as he did? More than that, he knew which judge to curry favor with, to joke with, defer to, overwhelm, even avoid. The criminal court was like a theater, Mickey had once explained to Laura. The more times you attend, the better you know the show. From judges to potential jurors to the entire police establishment, Mickey Horton knew them all. He liked them and they liked him.

At last when he was finally in a position to help his brother, his help was not wanted. All Bill had asked him to do was recommend another good criminal lawyer. So with a few in mind, he began asking around, only hoping that Bill's choice would be amenable to accepting his help, advice, and experience.

Chicago

When Kenton Davis received a message to call the chairman of the board of Woodridge Industries, he wondered what it was about. Could his old fraternity brother be after another charity donation? Or perhaps a pledge to speak at another of those devastatingly boring political functions? As a nationally known criminal defense attorney, Davis was constantly being bombarded with requests for speeches, free legal advice, and bail funds, and he had no desire to add to his already overloaded schedule. He wondered briefly if it might be a business call.

Feeling quite curious, Davis returned his old friend's call. "Hey, good buddy," he said into the phone jovially, "is this call professional or what?"

When he found out it was indeed professional, Davis signaled his law clerk to pick up the extension and take notes. Yes, he told Mickey, he knew Bill Horton was Mickey's brother. No, he had no idea why Mickey was requesting his services on behalf of Bill. Why wasn't Mickey taking his brother's case?

"He'll have to tell you about that himself," replied Woodridge's chairman of the board. "All I can do is provide his address and phone number. He'll be awaiting your call. The only reason he asked me to intervene is because you've become such a superstar that he felt you might never have taken a call from someone you didn't know and hadn't heard of."

When Davis hung up the phone, he asked his clerk, "Did you get all of that? What do you think?"

"We've had much more exciting cases. It isn't even a real murder, is it?"

Davis nodded. "The correct terminology, my boy, is homicide. That is undoubtedly what it is. The question is—what *degree* of homicide is it, and can I get him off?"

Davis gave Mickey a call to discuss Bill Horton's situation, then asked him if he wanted to be involved in the case.

"Yes," Mickey replied emphatically. "Very much, if you wouldn't mind. I intend to make myself and my staff available immediately. Bill and I have always been close and I want to do everything to help. It's Bill who has the reservations."

In the end, that little bit of mystery was what decided Davis to make the trip to Salem. Who knows? he told himself. I might even get enough material out of this case for another best-seller—as if you needed it. But even if this turns out to be a wild goose chase, so what? I can afford to take a chance on an out-of-the-way local case.

He told Mickey that he would make up his mind after he'd met with each of them.

Bill Horton and Kenton Davis entered the visitors' room simultaneously from different entrances, each sizing up the other before they were even seated. Davis was shorter and slighter than he appeared to be on television, Bill decided, then realized he'd mainly seen him when he was seated, being interviewed. He also had a slight limp, so it was clear that the natty cane he carried was not an affectation. His tweed jacket was British, his flannel slacks very preppy and his gleaming black oxfords looked hand-tooled. All very impressive, thought Bill as the men shook hands and sat down.

Davis got right down to business.

"Did you like your sister-in-law?"

"Not in the least."

"Could you clarify that?"

"My feelings toward her ranged from mild annoyance to absolute disgust."

"And the rest of your family, did they like her?"

"I would say that we all felt that way. Except for my brother Tommy, of course. He married her, so he must have seen something in her at one time. You'd have to ask *him* about that."

"Did you know that she had a heart condition?"

"Negative. Nobody knew, including her husband." Bill tensed, waiting for the question he knew was coming. He couldn't help but admire the elegant cut of Davis's clothes, his gold watch and ring. Mickey had once explained that you could invariably pick a criminal lawyer out of a lineup by his clothes—they were always classy. They had to be, Mickey had continued playfully, just so he could keep the jury awake during the interminable days of boring testimony.

Davis glanced down at his notes. "Her doctor upstate knew all right." Then he asked, "What were the two of you arguing about?"

Bill pointed to Davis's notes. "Don't you have *that* down there too?"

"No. As far as I can determine, most of what was said between you was not overheard." He looked carefully at Bill and detected a sigh of relief.

"Happy about that, huh?"

Bill shrugged but did not answer.

Davis made a show of shuffling through his notes. "What I have before me is an exemplary record of an outstanding young man at the height of his potential."

"Not quite," Bill corrected. "The height of my professional powers occurred over a year ago when I was perfecting new surgical techniques—"

"I have all of that here," Davis interrupted impatiently. "I know about that neurological problem with your right hand. I also know how you deferred a year of earnings to volunteer with the Red Cross, and I know just about everything else you've done. If you were an Eagle Scout or altar boy, my law clerks and researchers put it in here"—he tapped his notes—"and I know all about it."

Bill looked at him in amazement. "All that work before you've even decided to take my case?"

Davis smiled slightly. "That's right. And each evasion of yours helps me to arrive at my decision." He paused long enough, doing the usual trick, to make the defendant nervous. When Bill remained calm, he decided to take another tack. "Mickey has expressed interest in working with me. Of course, that's welcome news to you, I expect." Davis said casually, but he studied Bill carefully out of the corner of his eye.

"That all depends," Bill replied evasively.

"On exactly what?" Davis demanded.

Bill began to squirm uneasily. "You must understand that almost every Horton is touched by this. I don't want my family involved any more than they have to be. Acting in *my* behalf is not necessarily acting in *their* behalf."

Davis tapped his file and asked, "Are you fond of your brother?"

"Of course. I love him."

"And he, you?"

Bill nodded. "Mickey explained that he's simply extending a courtesy to an out-of-town attorney. He'll share his office, all the facilities, tell you what he knows about the judges, advise you on picking juries. He's told me all of that and I agree."

A big "but" hung in the air between them, and Davis picked up on it immediately. "But you don't want him in on my questioning of you, either here or in the court. You don't want to be forced to reveal what you and Kitty were arguing about."

With each point Davis made, Bill nodded vigorously.

"Did you mean to harm Kitty Horton in any way?"

"No, God help me. It was entirely accidental."

Davis shook his head. "Whether or not it was an accident is up to the court to decide. There's little doubt now that in the eyes of the law you killed her."

"Even if it was an accident?"

"If you were the driver of a car that ran someone over, and that person were declared dead *as a result*, you'd have killed that person." He paused, then added for emphasis, "Even if it were an accident."

Bill looked down at the floor and suppressed a shudder.

"The term *homicide* refers to the killing of one human being by another," Davis continued. "Sometimes, it can't be helped; it is a genuine accident. In other cases, when it could have been helped, it's considered unlawful—even though it was not planned and no malice was involved."

Davis gazed steadily at Bill, who seemed more interested in listening than in protesting his innocence. "Finally," he said, "we have murder in the first degree, by which we mean the unlawful and malicious, premeditated killing of one human being by another."

In spite of himself, Bill again shook his head vigorously.

"Deny it all you like, Dr. Horton," Davis snapped. "Without your help, there's little anyone can do to prove you didn't murder Kitty Horton. First, you yourself admit that you didn't like the woman. Second, she verbally accosted you. Third, you shook her with such strength and vigor that *she died as a result*. That strength and vigor could be interpreted as malice."

Bill looked up accusingly and cried, "You sound like a district attorney, or a hanging judge!"

Davis nodded and pounded the table for emphasis. "*Somebody* better sound like that, and now is none too soon. Your own counsel would be remiss if he were gentle and comforting and then led you into that den of lions. This, Dr. Horton, is what is known as *preparation*."

Bill put his head in his hands.

Slowly Davis began gathering his notes together, carefully replacing them in his attaché case. He lined up all his sharpened pencils, then swept them into a compartment at the bottom of the case. When he stood up, Bill rose too, and the two men shook hands.

"Thank you for coming and considering my case," Bill said in a subdued voice. "I want to cooperate in every way I can, short of hurting any innocent parties. Kitty had a mouth like a sewer. To repeat anything she said that day would be unforgivable."

"Wouldn't be worth it, huh?" Davis baited him. Bill shook his head. "Not worth your freedom? Not worth your license to practice?"

Bill shrugged. "I'll have to take my chances."

Davis sighed, realizing there was nothing more he could do for the time being. Besides, he had promised Mickey Horton that he'd drop over for a drink, and he was late already. He told Bill that Mickey would probably be calling him later. Bill gave him a charming, rueful smile and waved to him as he left the visitors' room.

Chapter Eleven

A Golden Silence

Davis stopped by the hotel desk to ask if he had any messages.

"Will you be spending another night with us, sir?" asked the desk clerk.

He shook his head and asked the clerk to prepare his bill, then arranged to have his packed bags checked behind the desk so he wouldn't have to carry them over to Mickey's. He phoned his office, followed through on some important calls, and had the desk clerk arrange his flight. Then he ordered a cab and reluctantly prepared himself for a duty call to his small-town colleague. A couple of hours of legal chatter about circuit courts and local bar associations would be about all he could take. He hoped the liquor would ease the going.

When Laura Spencer-Horton answered the door, she told him that Mickey had just called to say that he would be home in a few minutes and she hoped Davis wouldn't mind.

Mind? The woman was absolutely stunning. Her surroundings reflected her taste; her vocabulary hinted at her intelligence. But it was her face, figure, and utter charm that took his breath away. If this woman were the defendant, he would take the case in a minute. Guilt or innocence be damned, fee be damned, he would get her off—whatever the charge—and love every minute of it.

Laid out on the bar was his favorite single-malt Scotch, Bombay gin, some nuts, and some nice cheeses. Thank heaven, Davis thought, there were none of those ubiquitous dips and potato chips. He broke off a crusty chunk of French bread and spread cheese on it while Laura poured him a Scotch over ice, just the way he liked it. Before they sat together on the sofa, she brought everything over from the bar. Now that Davis was beginning to relax from his rather tense day, he realized that he was really hungry.

As a defense attorney, Davis was skilled at drawing out witnesses. As a clinical psychologist, Laura was equally skilled at drawing out patients' confidences. When Davis discovered that this stunning woman was a "shrink," he was even further impressed, and the two of them had a very genial, interesting conversation. In it he learned that Laura had once been engaged to Bill. He wondered fleetingly if Mickey were even taller and better-looking than Bill.

He got his answer when Mickey came bounding in, carrying his five-foot-nine frame briskly and walking with the wiry movements of a lightweight boxer. He had an engaging grin and a look of keen intelligence. Davis noticed that Laura was wearing flat shoes. In heels, he thought, she would have towered over Mickey.

After he kissed his wife, Mickey asked her how the baby was. With the classic pride of a new father, Mickey insisted not just on going right in to see his son, but on showing the baby off to his guest as well. Davis was obliged to follow the new parents into the nursery, where he looked down at a smiling boy with golden ringlets who reached up to touch Mickey's face. The baby was winsome, as Laura was, but any family resemblance ended there. Of Mickey, Davis could see no resemblance.

"His eyes used to be blue, but all babies' eyes are, they tell me," Mickey said proudly. "Now they're turning the Horton shade of hazel." Indeed they were. Then something popped into Davis's mind—he would be curious to compare this infant with baby pictures of Dr. Bill Horton. He did some quick mental arithmetic and realized, from what he could recall of his files, that Mickey could easily have been the father of this child. But he wasn't. Davis was certain of it.

As they returned to the living room, Mickey apologized for his overwhelming parental exuberance. "It's just that we waited and waited and tried everything . . . I was beginning to give up hope."

It figures, Davis thought to himself. He consented to stay to dinner, and while Laura went in to check on the food and Mickey changed, he looked at his files again and did some heavy figuring. He had dealt with enough schemers and liars to be able to read people quickly and expertly. He made rapid, cryptic notes to himself in his own indecipherable shorthand.

1. If baby Michael is not Mickey's, Mickey knows nothing about it. He has no suspicions whatsoever.

2. If Laura has any suspicions that the child is Bill's, she's not telling. She genuinely loves Mickey. She too wants me to defend Bill—whatever happened between them was probably a one-shot, an accident, whatever. In any case, she hasn't told Bill—or Mickey.

3. If the child is indeed Bill's, he is sure that Mickey has no idea and wishes to protect him. He also wishes to keep Laura from knowing that *he* knows.

4. All this secrecy is strangling Bill. He wishes to be the sacrificial goat in order to save the family. No one can talk him out of it. He risks first-degree murder by his silence.

5. The argument Bill refuses to talk about must have involved accusations from Kitty about his being the father of Laura's child. *He shook her to silence her*.

Soon Mickey rejoined Davis, having slipped into a comfortable pair of chinos, and before long dinner was served. Davis made sure all his notes had been safely tucked away, then joined Mickey and Laura at the table.

When Davis had accepted their dinner invitation, the couple had half interpreted it as a sign that he would take the case. Still they waited until he brought the subject up. This did not happen until after dinner, however, at which point Laura excused herself. The two men took some glasses of brandy into Mickey's study and began to talk.

"Do you have any idea what your brother and your sister-in-law fought about?" Davis asked. When Mickey shook his head, Davis snapped, "Come on, Counselor, you must have thought about it."

"Of course I have. We *all* have, the entire family. It must have involved the honor of the family. Kitty was a snoop and a great gossip. She would listen in on phone conversations, behind staircases, wherever. She had a malicious mouth. If she'd said something about Bill himself, it wouldn't have mattered very much. He's a macho kind of guy and pretty sure of himself. But if it meant protecting someone close to him, saving someone from getting hurt . . . well, that might have accounted for it."

"You realize that his silence may cost him a great deal," Davis observed quietly.

"Of course I do. We all do."

"I can prove that he didn't know about her heart condition. That in itself is apparent," Davis pointed out.

Mickey grinned. The "I can" was all the indication he needed—Davis was taking the case.

"That should get rid of the premeditated part. If you don't know you can shake her to death, then that's not your motive."

"What do you see as the worst we can expect?" Mickey asked anxiously.

Davis was relieved to hear the automatic "we." He'd need all the assistance he could get from Mickey. "We can't deny the anger. All the people who politely moved out of earshot watched him shake the dickens out of the woman. And I understand that the shouting rang through the corridors."

"That would have been Kitty only," Mickey insisted. "Bill doesn't shout. He doesn't *have* to."

Davis appreciated that as one of the finest compliments any brother could give to another. "Nevertheless," he continued, shaking his head, "the court will state that when he shook her, he committed a criminal act. He should never have laid a hand on her."

Mickey pulled out a box of cigars and offered one to Davis. "Well, Counselor, are we in business?"

Davis took a cigar and played with it before he recalled his doctor's orders. He put it down. "Without Bill's complete cooperation, it's going to be a real bruiser. All we can do is try."

They shook on it. Davis called the hotel and asked them to cancel his plane reservation, take his bags back to his room, and book him to stay on for another week, at least.

The trial itself followed Davis's game plan: hope for the best but realize that it's all in the bargaining. There had been enough witnesses at the time so that everything that had happened was duly retold in full. And so to make the bargain work for him Davis assembled a formidable collection of character witnesses from all over the country—all who had good things to say about Bill. Marcy Barnes, administrative head of the San Diego Red Cross, headed the California contingent. She brought with her testimony from every veteran who had been freely and generously treated by Dr. Bill Horton. Depositions arrived from surgeons too busy to attend but eager to acknowledge the importance of Bill's contributions to the field of surgery. Even the state's witnesses, who were called in to testify about Bill's attack on Kitty, defended him with great affection.

While the jury was out, Mickey asked Davis, "Well, what do you say? You can usually call these things."

Davis shrugged and grinned. "If this were a popularity contest, your brother would win hands down. I'm surprised he hasn't been nominated for a Nobel prize."

He sounded confident enough, but Mickey detected a note of equivocation in Davis's response that worried him.

Bill Horton was downstairs in the courtroom in a special temporary lockup. He had a surfeit of things to read—a stack of popular magazines on one side of him and a pile of medical journals on the other. But he had no inclination for reading just then—he had other things on his mind.

He had chosen not to testify in his own behalf and was now prepared to pay for it. He'd been surprised that Davis hadn't been more insistent on that. It was almost as if the man had somehow divined all that had happened, been concealed, denied, begrudged, and forgiven. He remembered when, after one particularly grueling session, Davis had mentioned meeting Tom Horton, Sr.

"I've finally met with your dad," he'd said lightly, "and we've had ourselves quite a long chat. He seems to know an awful lot about you." Davis had paused, peered closely at Bill, then added, "You know, it's a wise father who knows his own child."

Bill had been taken aback by the statement. He had immediately thought about baby Michael. Then, because he'd sensed that Davis was examining him for any change of expression, he'd deliberately changed the subject.

Now anxious and with heavy time to bide, he again thought about little Michael. He tried to picture him in his crib in his nursery. Abruptly he rose and began to pace in the confines of his cell. He'd never even seen the baby. He probably looks like every other baby, Bill told himself restlessly. If only Kitty hadn't said anything, he might never have guessed Michael was his.

If only Kitty hadn't said anything.

It was still an open question. There was no way he could know for sure if he was the father of Laura's child—unless he asked his father if Mickey had failed a sterility test.

But he would go to his grave before he asked his father that.

Fortunately, the death penalty was not an

issue in this case. After several hours the jury returned with a verdict of involuntary manslaughter. Bill stood before the judge awaiting sentence, his posture erect, his eyes clear, his face serene.

"This is a troubling sentence for me to impose, Dr. Horton," the judge began. "A man with your training, talents, and accomplishments should be free to work toward the greater good of the community. Nevertheless, you performed a criminal act in a fit of anger. To let you go would be negligence. An example must be set for the youth of this community. Someone with your advantages, education, and family background cannot be allowed to behave just as he wishes, whenever he wishes—without facing the consequences."

The judge paused a moment, then looked directly at Bill. "Therefore, I hereby impose the minimum sentence allowed me by law— which is two years imprisonment. With time off for good behavior, it can be considerably less."

Among those awaiting the verdict in court was Julie Olson. She had flown in to see the family and the new baby, only to find herself in the midst of a Horton family crisis. After Bill had been sentenced, she stayed around the courthouse long enough to hear Kenton Davis assure her grandparents that with time off for good behavior, Bill could expect to be out in six months. Goodness, she said to herself, that's less time than it took me to have a baby!

Nobody could get quite used to the svelte new Julie. She was tanned and thin and almost looked as if she'd grown an inch or two. "That would be most unusual considering you're in your late teens," Tom observed. "But I should have learned by now that *anything's* possible in my family!"

Back at the Horton house, after what the Hortons had been through in just the past few months, nobody knew whether to laugh or cry. Alice's instinct was to put out a batch of cookies and things for them to snack on. Following her grandmother's lead, Julie whipped out all the photographs she had taken in Palm Beach with Alva and her friends.

Sandy looked at each picture with awe. She had never seen so many beautiful people having so much fun. "Is that your boyfriend?" she asked eagerly, looking at a picture of her cousin with an absolutely gorgeous man. Julie only laughed.

When Alice was satisfied that everyone had been fed, she walked over to Julie and embraced her. At least I do *some* things right, she thought to herself. All had gone with Julie according to plan. As was the case with Sandy, everyone in Salem assumed that Julie had simply taken off close to a year to have a good time—first in Europe and then in Palm Beach. And Alice and her sister Martha had seen to it that no one would ever be able to guess that Julie had actually been close to home the entire time, giving birth to an illegitimate child, then putting it up for adoption. Far better that Julie be considered a socialite playgirl Alice decided firmly.

"Are you going to be staying here with Grandma, too?" Sandy asked hopefully. It seemed to her that her cousins were leading such exciting lives.

Julie shook her head, letting her long, newly streaked hair float about her shoulders in a shimmering cloud. "Nope," she replied with a smile. "I think even Grandma here would have to agree that I have joined the ranks of the grown-ups." Alice nodded. "I've got a brand-new life ahead of me, and I'd better find a place of my own, so I can settle in and let it all happen. And frankly, I can't wait!"

YOU CAN NOW ORDER PREVIOUS TITLES OF *SOAPS & SERIALS™* BOOKS BY MAIL

Just complete the order form and detach on the dotted line and send together with your check or money order payable to *SOAPS & SERIALS:*

SOAPS & SERIALS™
120 Brighton Road, Box 5201
Clifton, NJ 07015-5201

Please circle the books you wish to order:

THE YOUNG AND THE RESTLESS	BK #1 2 3
DAYS OF OUR LIVES	1 2 3
GUIDING LIGHT	1 2 3
ANOTHER WORLD	1 2 3
AS THE WORLD TURNS	1 2 3
CAPITOL™	1 2 3
DALLAS™	1 2 3
KNOTS LANDING™	1 2 3

Each book is $2.50 ($3.25 in Canada).

Total number of books circled _____
@ $2.50   ($3.25 Canada) $_____
Sales tax (CT residents only) $_____
Shipping and Handling $_____ .95
Total payment enclosed (checks or
money orders only) $_____

Name _____
Address _____ Apt. # _____
City _____
State _____ Zip _____
Telephone No. _____

DOOL3